Jeremy felt bliss spread to every part of his body…into his soul.

Her eyes were closed, and her lovely face glowed. He brushed her curls from her face and kissed her brow, her temple, unable to stop touching her.

For the first time in his life, his body had gone beyond the command of his mind. Odd, but he didn't feel a need for caution, as he usually did when a relationship threatened to become too intense. Instead, a welter of emotions coursed through him and he tried to sort them all out.

Tenderness?

Yeah.

Wonder?

That, too.

Confusion?

Definitely.

Dear Reader,

It is so difficult to leave a family, even a made-up one, whose lives I have been writing about for more than a year. From my own extended family as well as my husband's, I enjoy watching our young ones grow up and flex their wings, while they establish careers and find their special person. I just never get tired of a complicated (as all matters of the heart tend to be) love story and seeing the hero/heroine coming to grips with their personal demons as well as learning to trust their hearts... Uh-oh, I'm getting all choked up. Anybody got a hankie?

Best,

Laurie Paige

A PLACE TO CALL HOME

LAURIE PAIGE

SPECIAL EDITION®

Published by Silhouette Books

America's Publisher of Contemporary Romance

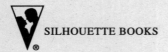 SILHOUETTE BOOKS

ISBN-13: 978-0-373-24806-3
ISBN-10: 0-373-24806-7

A PLACE TO CALL HOME

This edition published by arrangement with Harlequin Books S.A.

® and TM are trademarks of Harlequin Books S.A., used under license. Trademarks indicated with ® are registered in the United States Patent and Trademark Office, the Canadian Trade Marks Office and in other countries.

Visit Silhouette Books at www.eHarlequin.com

Printed in U.S.A.

Books by Laurie Paige

Silhouette Special Edition

*Home for a Wild Heart #828
*A Place for Eagles #839
*The Way of a Man #849
*Wild Is the Wind #887
*A River To Cross #910
**Something To Talk About #1396
†Showdown! #1532
†The One and Only #1545
†Found in Lost Valley #1560
‡Romancing the Enemy #1621
†The Devil You Know #1641
†A Kiss in the Moonlight #1654
†The Other Side of
    Paradise #1708
§Second-Time Lucky #1770
§Under the Western Sky #1781
§Acquiring Mr. Right #1792
§A Place To Call Home #1806

Silhouette Romance

††Cara's Beloved #917
††Sally's Beau #923
††Victoria's Conquest #933
*A Rogue's Heart #1013

*Wild River
**The Windraven Legacy
†Seven Devils
‡The Parks Empire
§Canyon Country
††All-American Sweethearts

LAURIE PAIGE

"One of the nicest things about writing romances is researching locales, careers and ideas. In the interest of authenticity, most writers will try anything… once." Along with her writing adventures, Laurie has been a NASA engineer, a past president of the Romance Writers of America, and is a mother and a grandmother. She was twice a Romance Writers of America RITA® Award finalist for Best Traditional Romance and has won awards from *Romantic Times BOOKreviews* for Best Silhouette Special Edition and Best Silhouette, in addition to appearing on the *USA TODAY* bestseller list. Recently resettled in Northern California, Laurie is looking forward to whatever experiences her next novel will provide.

Dedicated to all those who have reached a certain age, in which case it's "about the diamonds."

Chapter One

Zia Peters couldn't have been more startled when the familiar voice of Jeremy Aquilon greeted her outside the Residential Hotel of Vernal, Utah, as she climbed wearily out of her compact car.

"Jeremy," she said blankly, staring as if she couldn't quite recall who he was and managing to drop her keys and purse at the same time.

But of course she did know him. He was part of her "blended" family. When Jeremy's uncle, Jeff, had taken in Jeremy and his two younger stepcousins—the cousins, a brother and sister, were underage and wards of the state—her mother had been assigned to the case...and ended up married to the orphans' guardian.

That had been fourteen years ago. While her mother

had fitted in perfectly with the Aquilons, Zia, at nineteen, hadn't felt part of their family, or any family, not since her dad had walked out when she was four.

She summoned a smile as Jeremy stopped beside her. "What are you doing here?" she asked, the surprise obvious in her voice, not to mention other emotions she couldn't define. She picked up her purse and tossed the keys inside.

"Waiting for you?" he suggested with a humorous lilt in his smooth baritone.

He had no idea how those words reached down and stirred a pot of turbulent emotion inside her. No one waited for her, and that was a fact. Chiding herself for the flash of self-pity, she maintained a pleasant expression, aware that his appearance was having a keen impact on her senses.

His hair gleamed shiny black in the sun as he ambled down the porch steps. The June breeze lifted the perpetual wave that curved over his forehead. The wayward lock looked silky soft as he brushed it to the side, unlike the hard, sinewy lines of his six-two body.

The playful wind also carried the scent of balsam and aftershave, as if he'd recently stepped out of the shower. His jawline, strong and angular, was smoothly shaved. An instinctive urge to test that smoothness had her drawing back in shock at the impulse.

His face was tanned from days working in the sun, his eyes were dark and he exuded a controlled masculinity, a quiet assurance that hinted at thoughts not spoken, depths not plumbed. All her friends had found him intriguing on the infrequent occasions when she and Jeremy had visited the Aquilon home at the same time during their college years.

As a civil engineer working for the state of Utah, he supervised the building of roads and bridges. She knew him as an unruffled solver of life's problems, large or small. He'd come to the rescue of his cousins when he'd hardly been more than a boy himself, and he'd helped her through a rough patch once, a time that she'd rather forget. Neither of them ever referred to it.

Sorrow and regret, mixed with shame, embarrassment and other feelings too painful to sort out, flashed through her.

She shoved aside the emotions and popped open the trunk of her car. Matching his amused tone, she quipped, "Your crystal ball works better than mine. I wasn't sure what time I was going to make it in due to all the road construction going on."

"It's summer. We have to get as much done as possible."

He shrugged and reached past her to lift out her largest piece of luggage as if it weighed no more than her overnight case, which she removed from the trunk. He also took the medium one before she could grab it, his arm brushing hers as he did.

"Seriously, how did you know I was coming today?" she asked.

"Seriously," he replied, still with the note of humor, "your mom called just before I left the office. She said you'd called on your cell phone and reported you were about thirty miles from town but stuck in traffic. She was worried you wouldn't get in before dark. I told her the delay wasn't more than fifteen minutes." He paused. "I said I'd make sure you arrived okay."

His gaze took in the last rays of sunlight on the western horizon before returning to her.

Suppressing annoyance that her mother had thought it necessary to contact Jeremy and ask him to check on her, she said brightly, "I'm fine." She hesitated, then added, "I thought you were working on a bridge in the Desolation Canyon area."

She knew he had a cabin near town, one he'd bought three years ago and was remodeling as he got time. Normally, he lived in an RV or temporary barracks at the construction site while on a job. Her new position as the county curriculum director would keep her busy at the school headquarters in town. She figured they wouldn't run into each other often.

"Do you have a project in this area now?" she asked when he didn't say anything.

His grin was brilliant enough to stop traffic. "You might say so. Vernal is the DOT's district headquarters for this region, and I'm the new district manager. I'll be at the office a lot, except when I'm in the field checking on progress. Or problems, as the case may be."

DOT was the Department of Transportation. She hadn't realized they would have a regional office in a town of eight thousand people. Industry here mostly consisted of services for travelers on Highway 40, the government offices of the county seat, businesses serving the ranchers, Indian reservations and forestry service in the surrounding area or outfitters catering to adventurers who came for fishing, hunting or rafting through Desolation Canyon on the Green River.

The biggest attraction was Dinosaur National Monument which straddled the border between Utah and Colorado. A huge pink dinosaur on Main Street welcomed people to the town.

"That's wonderful," she said sincerely. "Congratulations on the promotion. Uh, did you mention this when we were home for the wedding two weeks ago?"

He shook his head. "Truthfully, I didn't think I had a chance at the position, so there was no point in talking about it."

His stepcousin, Krista, had married into a very old, very wealthy Colorado family on the first Saturday of June.

Zia truly hoped the twenty-five-year-old found happiness in her marriage. Krista, an eleven-year-old when Jeff and Caileen wed, had readily welcomed Zia as a roommate when Zia had visited during college breaks.

Hero worship was something she didn't deserve, but Krista hadn't known that. The girl had been sweet and trusting and had asked Zia for advice as a youngster would of a much-admired older friend. If only she'd been the person Krista thought she was—wise and generous and kind. If only she could turn back the clock and be that person. Yeah, if only….

Zia sighed as she headed for the hotel lobby to sign in.

"Tired?" Jeremy asked companionably.

He was being polite. She knew that, but for a second, she pictured a different welcome, one in which the man of her dreams rushed out to greet her and sweep her into his arms in a loving embrace, happy to be with her again.

Since the wedding, with Krista so radiant and Lance so filled with adoration each time he'd looked at his bride, Zia had experienced a restless yearning that reached all the way to her soul or some place of deep, dark misery.

Where was the special person who would love her like that? Did he even exist, she questioned the part of her that sometimes, as at the wedding, longed for romance and fulfillment. Her eyes burned with sudden tears.

Heavens, but she was at a low point today, *not* a good time for a welcoming committee of any kind, even one as considerate as Jeremy.

"A little," she admitted. "It was super of you to come by. As soon as I'm in my room, I'll call the folks to let them know I made it okay." She sounded briskly dismissive. "I'm sorry," she immediately added. "I didn't mean to be abrupt. I'm not very good company right now."

"You probably need food," he said in his unruffled manner. He glanced at his wristwatch. "How about if I come back in an hour or so and take you to the best steak house in town?"

What could she say to such a gracious offer but yes?

Besides, her mother would be appalled if she acted like a total ass to Jeremy. Truly, she didn't mean to be unfriendly, but she really was weary. What should have been an easy drive from Provo, where she'd been supervisor of federal educational programs, to Vernal had taken several extra hours due to construction delays.

"Give me an hour and a half," she requested. "I'm going to soak in a hot tub for a while before I do anything else."

"Good idea." He placed the large bag and the medium-size one on a luggage carrier inside the lobby before giving her a half wave, then headed out the door.

Zia sighed again and went to the front desk. "I'm Zia Peters. I have a reservation."

"Welcome, Miss Peters," the young woman behind the desk greeted her, her fingers busy on the computer as she pulled up the file. "I'm Rachel, your day host. You're staying with us for two weeks?"

"Yes. Maybe more. I'll be looking for an apartment, so I'm not sure how much time I'll need."

"No problem. Just let us know as soon as possible if you want extra time. Hmm, actually I can give you a better rate if you agree to stay a month. If you have to change the time span later, it's no problem."

The price break was a twenty percent discount, and Zia figured it would take at least a month to find a place. "Great. Let's plan on a month."

After filling out the forms and putting the charges on her credit card, she rolled the luggage cart to her room, pleased that it was on the ground floor and had a door opening onto the side porch as well as one to the inner corridor.

The queen bed fit into an alcove to the left of the sitting room. The bathroom was on that side, too. A tiny kitchen nestled into another niche, along with a closet, on the opposite wall.

Windows flanked the door to the porch, giving her a view of eastern hills, sagebrush and a line of chokecherries, salt cedars and willows along an arroyo.

She quickly hung her clothing in the closet, stored her other items in the dresser drawers, then ran a bath. While the tub was filling, she called her mom. "Hi, I'm in," she said when her mother answered.

"Oh, good. You had such a long day, I was worried about you falling asleep at the wheel."

Zia had gotten up early to let the movers collect her possessions and put them in storage until she got settled in her new place. The packing and loading had taken longer than planned, so she hadn't hit the road until midafternoon. The traffic delays had added to the length of the trip.

"I'm fine," she assured her mom.

"Did you see Jeremy?"

"Yes. He was here at the hotel when I arrived. We're going to dinner later. At the best steak house in town," she added.

"Good," her mother said, her tone rich with approval.

Jeremy had always been hardworking and responsible and clear-thinking…all the things she'd had trouble with while growing up, all the things that brought on regret whenever she was reminded of the past.

She determinedly put the thought out of her mind. "Got to go," she said brightly. "I want to take a hot bath and relax before we go to dinner."

"Have a good time. Give Jeremy our love."

"I will. Love you. Bye for now."

She closed the cell phone, near despair or something equally gloomy. What *was* the matter with her? It had to be more than the wedding and the emotion associated with it, but what?

This move was supposed to be a good thing—sensible, logical, great for her career.

Except she hadn't expected to see Jeremy the moment she arrived. After the long, hard day, she hadn't been prepared to face him, just as she hadn't been prepared for the turmoil inside when she'd danced with him at his cousin's wedding.

Jeremy in jeans was appealing. Jeremy in a tux had been "awesome," as one of Krista's friends had said at the reception.

He really had been gorgeous. If Hollywood needed a new James Bond, he would be first on her list.

Shaking her head, she reminded herself she was no longer a teenager in an emotional and hormonal uproar, then stripped out of her jeans and T-shirt and headed for the tub.

"Ahh," she groaned upon sinking into pleasantly hot water nearly up to her neck. She'd set the radio alarm for thirty minutes so she could relax completely without keeping an eye on the clock before facing the evening.

Zia sprang upright when the alarm went off. She'd tried meditation techniques, but she hadn't relaxed at all during the soak although she'd given it her best.

Memories had returned to haunt her as they some-times did when she was tired or tense or both. Seeing Jeremy had brought it all back—those days when every moment had seemed of earthshaking importance, when the world had revolved around her and her friends and their hectic lifestyle.

Or so she had thought.

She'd learned a harsh lesson the year she and Sammy broke up. The love of her young life had been horrified when she'd told him she was pregnant. While she wasn't sure why the birth control pills had failed, other than she'd had a terrible cold and stomach flu that spring, she hadn't seen it as a huge problem. Although a college dropout, Sammy had had a good job in construction.

Just as her father had at the same age. Now her dad owned his own construction company and made lots of money. True, that had happened much later in his life, but she'd envisioned her and Sammy working together and making their marriage a huge success...as opposed to her parents' failure.

Why had she thought she was so much smarter and more capable than her mom had been at her age?

The confidence, or arrogance, of youth, she answered the question and surprisingly again felt the quick sting of remorse as she considered her mother's life.

Caileen had dropped out of college and married at nineteen. Zia had been born ten months later. They had lived in a van, traveling around the country to the best surfing spots, her mom working at odd jobs while her dad did construction.

After nearly five years of roaming, her mom had moved into an apartment and worked for the university while finishing her degree in counseling. She'd also worked as a dishwasher at a local restaurant at night. The boss had let her bring her child with her. Some of Zia's earliest memories were of sleeping in the storage room off the kitchen, surrounded by huge cans of food and hundred-pound sacks of potatoes.

She found herself smiling at that memory while an ache settled in her heart. Odd, to be so emotionally unsettled today.

Taking a new job as curriculum planner and coordinator for the county was a step up for her, one she was excited about, but a big responsibility. Perhaps that was the reason she felt so nervy.

She dressed in navy-blue slacks and a white shell, then laid out a long-sleeved shirt to take with her since the desert nights were usually cool at this elevation, which was over five thousand feet. She twisted her hair up on the back of her head and secured it with a butterfly clip before putting on a light foundation, eyeliner and rose-hued lipstick.

She still had twenty minutes, so she settled in a floral-covered rocking chair to wait, her thoughts once more on the past.

Six months after her fourth birthday, her parents had separated. They'd quarreled over money, over staying in one place, over her, over everything that touched their lives. Her fun, surfer-king father had walked out.

It had taken a long time to forgive her mother for that,

and even longer to realize her dad had also made a choice and that it hadn't included his wife and daughter. It wasn't until she was alone, pregnant and worried about the future that she'd understood something of what her mother had gone through while trying to provide a healthy, stable home for a child who was asthmatic—thank goodness she'd outgrown that malady—and having to count every penny, plus getting in study time, too.

How had she withstood the stress and pressure and loneliness of those years?

Closing her eyes and resting her head on the chair back, Zia felt the familiar regret at her impatient defiance of Caileen's rules and advice against a serious involvement during her first year of college. All the signs of Sammy's self-absorption had been there, as her mom had pointed out, but she'd refused to see them. She'd been pretty self-centered, too.

Ah, well. What was done, was done.

She'd been foolish and naive at nineteen. At thirty-three, she hoped she was wiser. And a better person—

A knock on the outside door interrupted her musing.

Jeremy felt he could do no less than invite Zia out to dinner on her first night in town, especially since her mom had called and asked him to make sure Zia arrived okay. He would do anything for Caileen and his uncle Jeff, who had formed the stable home base every kid needed while growing up. His feelings for them ran deep.

Zia, on the other hand, had always seemed rather

remote and aloof. However, he hadn't been around her all that much, so he really couldn't say. After Jeff and Caileen had married, Zia had gone to live in another state and work in her father's construction company office while attending the university there. She and her mom hadn't been getting along at the time.

In the fall, he'd left, too, going to the university in Boise on a math scholarship. Now, fourteen years later, it looked as if he and Zia were going to be residents of the same town. He wondered briefly if this would be a problem, but decided there was no reason for their lives to overlap more than in the past.

After finding out which room Zia was in, Jeremy went to the outside door and knocked. She answered at once.

As usual, her stunning beauty—five-nine, slender physique, long naturally blond hair, blue eyes—made his throat close for a second. The same thing had happened when he'd first seen her.

As a high school senior, he'd taken a college history course, intent on getting out on his own as soon as he finished his schooling. Zia had been in the class. That first day, all the guys had nearly fallen out of their chairs when she walked in with a friend, laughing and talking, seemingly unconscious of the picture she made.

He had to give her that. While most women would have used such great natural beauty to their advantage, Zia acted indifferent to hers.

At the time, he'd had no idea their lives would become entangled before the school year was over.

"Hello," she said, opening the door and pulling him back into the present.

Her scent enveloped him as he returned her greeting. While her perfume was sometimes floral, as at the wedding, or sometimes on the spicy side, as now, there was always a hint of freshness about her, as if she embodied springtime.

"You were right about needing food." she told him with a rueful grimace. "I skipped lunch, then ate cheese crackers while sitting in traffic. Now I'm starved."

He nodded at her small talk and waited while she gathered her purse and a shirt for the evening, then escorted her to the four-wheel drive SUV so necessary for his work in a country of deep canyons, dry washes and towering mesas.

"The Green River steak house is a local favorite. We try to keep it a secret from outsiders," he said after they were on their way.

"I promise not to tell anyone about it."

He smiled and relaxed at the mock seriousness of her quip. She was in a better humor now than when she'd first arrived. He'd always felt that she avoided him whenever possible…well, actually she avoided the entire family other than very brief visits on special occasions, such as being asked to take part in the wedding as Krista's maid of honor.

For a second his insides tightened painfully as he envisioned the angel dressed in blue who came down the aisle before the bride. He'd hardly been able to tear his gaze away. Odd, but in some ways, it was almost as if

Zia hadn't been present, as if her spirit had fled and left only the incredibly lovely husk of her body to carry out her duties.

When he'd danced with her at the reception, she'd stared over his shoulder at some distant view invisible to lesser mortals. He'd puzzled over her remote attitude, but if she preferred to remain aloof from the rest of them, it was her loss.

However, later, before Krista and Lance left on their honeymoon, he'd overheard Zia whisper, "Be happy, Krista. Find something in each day to bring joy to you and Lance."

When they waved the couple off, he'd caught an expression of intense...loneliness? grief?...in her eyes for a second, then she'd walked away from the crowd of well-wishers and headed for her car as if she couldn't wait to flee.

Against his will, he recalled blue eyes that had once looked like bruises in a face so pale he'd been afraid she was going to die on him.

He sucked in a harsh breath as a gang of tiny darts hit his heart all at once, making him aware that he'd once been truly worried for the lovely woman seated beside him, who normally kept up a pleasant facade and rarely gave a hint of her own deeper feelings. Ignoring the softer part of himself that still felt sorry for her in some ways, he pulled into a parking space and went around to help her out of the SUV.

"This is lovely," she said.

He stopped when she did and gazed at the colors of

the sunset, all gold and magenta, highlighting the sky beyond the mesa country that dominated the horizon.

"Yes," he said, but his eyes had returned to her.

He mentally muttered a curse at the attraction he couldn't deny. Okay, she was gorgeous, but beauty is as beauty does.

When he'd first met Zia, she'd been headstrong, thoughtless and self-centered. In his opinion. But that was long ago. In all fairness, he admitted he really didn't know her as an adult.

Taking her arm, he ushered her inside where they were led to a table next to the window.

"A full panoramic view," she said in approval. "I love the colors of a desert sunset, don't you?"

He answered with a grunt of agreement and accepted the menu the hostess handed him.

He observed her over the edge of the menu. There was something different about her, he decided, feeling the annoying little darts again, something sad or perhaps nostalgic. Maybe she was remembering the past, too.

"I can recommend the prime rib," he said, bringing them back to the mundane present.

They both ordered the prime rib special. He selected a red wine, a merlot that he recalled she liked.

"The wedding was lovely, wasn't it?" she said after the wine had been served, along with a basket of hot bread.

"The bride and groom are probably at their computers as we speak, going over contracts," he said, grinning.

Her laughter was unexpected, a gift reaching right

down into his chest. Now where had that strange idea come from?

"I'm surprised they're taking a month for a honeymoon. But I'm glad they are," she added thoughtfully.

"I don't think it matters. Both of them are such workaholics, they would probably rather be up to their ears in one of their projects than anywhere else. I still have trouble seeing Krista as a hard-nosed businesswoman."

"Ah, but you didn't hear her tell the florist that if he wanted any future orders from the Aquilons, he'd better fulfill the agreement they had and pronto! He came up with the rest of the floral arrangements with no delays."

When they chuckled together, he felt tension flow out of him. So, the dinner was going to go okay. After tonight, he would be busy with his new job and she would be engrossed in hers.

For a second, he wondered if fate was playing some diabolical trick on them, bringing them to the same town at the same time via the promotions. Caileen had been glad, but he thought that was because she was a mother with one chick, and that chick was very beautiful...not to mention distant and rather standoffish.

Maybe that was why she hadn't married, which was another reason her mother worried about her. At the wedding reception, he'd heard Caileen whisper to his uncle that she hoped Zia would find someone soon.

"Aren't you rather young to be a district manager?" Zia asked, breaking into his thoughts.

Irritation washed over him, but he gave her a lazy smile while slightly tipping his glass toward her. "I'm only three months younger than you and you're the school curriculum director for the whole county."

"That's not as impressive as being a district manager on the state level. I was wondering at the responsibility...but then, you've never been afraid to take on any amount of responsibility, have you?"

Blue eyes met his, and for a moment, he knew they were both remembering another place and another night that now seemed more of a nightmare than reality. He pushed the memory back into the black box of the past.

"You were seventeen when you ran away with Tony and Krista and lived on your own for a year. I still don't see how you kept from starving."

"In the summer, we lived off the land. I worked in a grocery store during the winter. I got all the discarded produce I wanted for free. A few bruises on the apples didn't bother us."

"You made up the year you lost in record time and graduated from college the same year I did. You were taking classes in high school and college at the same time. Remember that history class we were both in?"

"Yeah. I was in a hurry to get started."

"With what?" she asked softly, a sardonic note in her voice.

"My career. My life," he added for no good reason that he could think of.

"Life," she echoed and her eyes went dark, as if she'd thought of something that made her unhappy.

The horde of darts pricked at him. He shrugged them off. Whatever her life was, it was of her own making.

He had a full plate with his new position and the problems that went with it.

After the tender beef and baked potato dinner, he ordered coffee while she asked for tea with milk and brown sugar. He recalled that she preferred the tea over dessert, that she rarely ate dinner rolls and never indulged in something so decadent as butter. However, she loved brownies with pecans and had always praised Krista to the skies when she made them for her.

He wondered why he remembered something like that about her when there were other, more shattering things to muse on. He'd never asked, not then and not once in the intervening years, why she'd called him for help that night long ago. The night she'd lost the child she carried.

Chapter Two

It had been eerily dark that night, with only a sliver of moon showing beyond the trees lining the creek. Jeremy had answered Zia's summons as quickly as possible, not sure what to expect. She'd said she needed a ride when she'd called him.

He parked his secondhand pickup in front of the cabin. The old fishing camp, part of a state park now, wasn't going to be opened until extensive renovations were done to the cottages. Since the repairs hadn't been started yet, he figured it would be a while before they were used again.

No other vehicles were around. Through a crack in the ancient cabin's curtains, he could detect a light.

Zia.

His insides tightened as he got out and gently closed the door. He wondered why she'd called him. It wasn't as if they were close or anything, even if his uncle and her mother did have something going between them.

So what could Zia's call for help mean?

Forcing a calm he was far from feeling, he went to the cabin door and softly knocked. "Zia? It's me, Jeremy."

"Wait," he heard her say in a strange voice, a hoarse whisper as if she were being strangled.

His nerves tightened as the seconds clicked by, then he heard the slide bolt being drawn back. He turned the knob and went inside. Zia, looking like hell and much older than her nineteen years, stared at him, her eyes the only color in her face.

"What is it?" he asked as she sat on the rumpled sleeping bag spread over the steel frame of a cot.

She pressed her lips together, then leaned forward, her hands gripping her knees, obviously in pain. Beneath the T-shirt and leggings she wore, he saw her abdominal muscles contract as if in a spasm. His insides tightened, too. He didn't know what was going on, but he knew it wasn't good.

He settled beside her and put an arm around her shoulders. Pulling her hair into a bundle, he held it at the back of her neck so he could observe her face. "What's happening?"

"Miscarriage," she said. "I think."

A shiver ran down his back. While he'd taken a first aid course, he wasn't equipped for this type of emergency. He held her until the contraction subsided, until she sighed and pulled slightly away and gazed at him.

"Thanks for coming." Her smile was weak, apologetic. "You were the only person I could think of...the only one I trusted."

"Shouldn't we go to the hospital or something?" he asked, wondering where all her elite, sophisticated friends were. She was part of the "in" crowd at the university.

"In a minute," she said and gasped, bending forward from her waist and grasping her knees again. "Help me to the bathroom."

He cupped an arm around her waist and half carried her into the adjoining room. Sweat trickled down his scalp, his chest, his back.

She gave him a weary, rueful glance from eyes that looked like bruised petals. He stepped back into the other room, leaving the door ajar in case she needed him.

Peering into the dingy mirror, she combed her hair and pulled it back with a stretchy band, then splashed water on her face. Little curling tendrils formed around her face, making her look as vulnerable as eleven-year-old Krista. Her audible sigh dipped right down inside him.

When she came out, he slipped an arm around her waist and helped her to the cot. Following her instructions, he gathered her belongings and erased all signs of her having been in the cabin. He stored the stuff in the truck and came back for her.

"Let me rest a minute, then we'll go," she said, then with a brief smile, she added, "Poor Jeremy. After donating blood and saving my life, are you worried that you'll have to take care of me for the rest of your life?"

"The thought never entered my mind."

That was the truth. She'd been a spectator at an illegal drag race a couple of months ago. The cars had side-swiped each other and a piece of chrome had flown off and hit her in the neck. It was one of those freakish moments life liked to throw at a person. He and his uncle, being O-negative in blood type, had been called by the hospital to help replace the large amount of blood she'd lost.

At the time, he hadn't known their lives would become entangled due to family ties, he mused as he took a sip of coffee and returned to the present and the restaurant, aware of glances their way from other patrons. Zia drew attention wherever she went although, as usual, she seemed unaware of it.

He stared at the scar on the side of her neck, still visible above the collar of the shirt all these years later.

"I wore turtlenecks for the rest of that year so no one could see the scar," she said, her eyes following his line of sight as she added milk and sugar to the cup of steaming tea.

"Sorry, I didn't mean to stare." He looked at the sky, now a dark blue with a crystal drop of teal clinging to the horizon.

"You were remembering the past," she said. "I was, too. It was terrible of me to put you in such a position. I didn't know who else to call."

"I wondered why you didn't call Sammy."

Her lovely face became solemn with a disillusionment she'd never before allowed to surface in his presence. "He'd already walked out on me once. I would hardly give him a chance to do so again. My best friend had driven me to the cabin and promised not to tell anyone where I was. I didn't want to call her out in the middle of the night. Her parents would have questioned her if they'd heard her leaving at that hour."

"So that left me."

"Yes." She sipped the tea, then gazed at him over the rim of the cup, the steam adding a mysterious aura to her eyes. "I've tried not to bother you with my woes since then."

"Have there been other problems?" he asked.

She shook her head. Wispy curls floated around her temples. He remembered how soft her hair had been the one time he'd touched it. Sometime past midnight of that night long ago, he'd taken her to a twenty-four hour clinic where she'd been checked out and pronounced fine. The doctor had told them that over fifty percent of first pregnancies ended in miscarriage.

"Just the body's way of preparing for the real thing," he'd assured them in a hearty manner, treating them as a couple.

Neither he nor Zia had explained the truth. Between the two of them, they had managed to pay the bill. Later he'd received a check from Zia for his share. Two words had been written on the accompanying note. "Thanks forever."

"Actually my life is quite calm and peaceful. Just the way I like it." Her smile was droll.

He smiled, too. "Same here."

"No serious involvement to give you heart pains?" she teased, surprising him with the question.

He grimaced. The woman he'd been dating had made it clear she wasn't interested in moving from Cedar City in the southwestern part of the state to another small town in the northeastern section, so that had ended the relationship. "None. You?"

Her smile dimmed a bit. "I was going pretty steady with a high school teacher in Provo when this job offer came up. When he didn't get down on his knees and beg me to stay, I was disappointed. Then I realized the promotion meant more to me than he did."

"You didn't love him," Jeremy murmured.

"I cared about him, but I didn't want a lifelong commitment." Her eyes seemed to darken. "I'm not sure I ever will."

"You can't let a jerk like Sammy influence the rest of your relationships," he advised.

"No, I haven't. At least, I don't think I have." She sighed. "Mom's worried, though. She made some strong hints during the wedding festivities that I might be too picky. I didn't remind her that her first attempt at marriage ended in divorce."

"Is that what you're afraid of?"

"I'm not afraid of anything," she said, her tone cooler. "Sorry. I didn't mean to sound sharp. I just haven't met *the one,* I suppose."

"Yeah, same here."

"All my friends thought you were a hunk," she

murmured on a determinedly lighter note. "They kept dropping by the house when we were home on vacations. Did you notice?"

He shook his head. "I was concentrating too hard on getting my courses in, making decent grades and graduating. Nothing was going to stand in my way."

"That's what my mother said I should do when I was going with Sammy. I've never had the courage to tell her she was right."

"It was a long time ago," Jeremy advised, catching a hint of regret in her manner. "We were young."

"Young," she echoed, brushing back a curl from her cheek. "And foolish. Why do those two go together so easily?"

When she laughed, he did, too. But he didn't share the irony. He felt sorry for her. She'd learned a hard lesson in trust, one she'd obviously never forgotten. However, that was neither here nor there. He felt he could truthfully report to her mom that Zia was safe and well in her new environment.

"Ready to go?" he asked as she patted back a yawn.

Zia studied the three-story building where she would be working come August. She had seven weeks to find a place to live, get her furniture out of storage and settle in. That should be plenty of time.

Meanwhile, she was reading over all her books on continuous courses of study for students from first to twelfth grade.

Research had shown that more than about six weeks

off from school and the kids forgot a lot of what they had learned. That meant teachers had to spend at least a month reviewing old material before beginning new stuff each and every school year.

She wanted to decrease the review time to two weeks and hoped to make changes in the scheduling of the semesters, too.

A vehicle pulled into the parking space next to her. Startled, she glanced around to see Jeremy in the SUV.

He rolled down the window. "Checking out your new domain?"

She nodded, feeling a little shy because he'd read her so easily. "I wanted to see where the building was located and how the town was laid out."

"Where's your car?"

"I walked down from the hotel. I needed the exercise after spending all those hours in traffic yesterday."

"Good thinking. I'm heading for the bridge site south of here, down toward Desolation Canyon. I saw you when I pulled out of the parking lot at the DOT building and wondered if you'd like to go along. The scenery is pretty nice."

The educational offices were across the street from the courthouse. The squat building down from the courthouse was the one he pointed out as the DOT regional headquarters. She hadn't realized it would be near her workplace.

"You probably don't want to be trapped in a car again after your long trip yesterday," Jeremy said when she failed to respond.

She turned to him. "Sorry, I was thinking about work.

If you're sure I won't be in the way, I'd love a scenic tour of the area," she said on an impulse she couldn't quite explain.

"Hop in," he invited with an engaging smile.

As they drove out of town, she had to chuckle at the dinosaur that welcomed visitors.

"Yeah," Jeremy said. "It takes some getting used to."

"Why pink?"

"Beats me."

It was nice, she realized, to laugh with him, to have someone to be at ease with. Jeremy was the only person who knew all the ugly details of her secret past, so she didn't have to be on guard with him every minute the way she was with her family and friends back in Idaho. In fact, she hadn't really been free and easy with anyone in ages, perhaps not since she was nineteen.

That was the past, she reminded herself hastily. When she'd agreed to take the new position, she'd decided the move would be a starting point, a new day in her life. Regret and mistakes would be wiped out, and she'd start over with a clean slate.

Could that be done? Her emotional upheaval since the wedding had upset those grand schemes, and now she was unsure she'd done the correct thing.

Her gaze was drawn to her companion. What an irony that the one person who knew all the details of her foolish, betrayed heart should be here, reminding her of long-ago dreams and the confidence she'd once had in them.

"Look," he said softly, pointing out the rugged view in front of the truck. "The Uinta Mountains of this area are unique in that they run east-west rather than north-south like most ranges. We also have eleven peaks over thirteen-thousand feet. King's Peak, at 13,498, is the highest in the state." He paused. "Am I boring you with the travelogue?"

"Not at all. I like knowing about the area where I live. Most people don't realize there are canyons and cliffs up here that are as impressive as the Grand Canyon."

"Yeah, Desolation Canyon of the Green River for one. It's a prime rafting area."

"Have you gone down it in a raft?"

"Several times. It's fun."

"If you like life-threatening adventure," she murmured wryly.

His chuckle was low and husky. Intimate. It sent a funny sensation down her spine. Being with Jeremy, away from their common environment, put a different angle on their knowing each other, as if the past was too far away to count.

She frowned as an uneasy feeling disturbed her pleasure with the scenery. She wasn't an adventurer, she decided. She liked life to be predictable and stable. She no longer considered living in a van and following the best surf to be the height of fun as she had as a four-year-old. She was no longer positive she knew everything worth knowing as she had been at nineteen.

Young and foolish? Yeah, been there, done that.

When he pulled off the road at a vista point, she got out of the SUV and stood on the lookout, wary and disturbed.

To the west rose the Badland cliffs. To the east was

the gorge of the river. She and Jeremy stood on a mile-high plateau between the two. A breeze from the canyon caressed their faces, cooling the heat that enveloped her when he moved near.

"Look," he said, speaking close to her ear, "I think there's a bighorn on that bluff."

She saw a white spot moving in the distance. The mountain sheep clambered up the steep incline and disappeared over the ridge.

"How do they manage such slopes?" she asked in awe.

"Suction cups for feet, I think."

His breath touched her temple as he laughed. Instinctively she turned her face to his as amusement caught her unawares. She sucked in a quick, startled breath as she realized their lips were only inches apart. And that she wanted...

His eyes, which had some surprising green flecks near the pupil, locked on hers as if he could read that internal yearning. For a second that seemed an eternity, they stared at each other.

He stepped back. "We'd better move on. It's a short distance to the site but very winding."

They were mostly silent on the rest of the trip, other than her exclaiming over each new panoramic view, which seemed to occur with each bend in the road.

When they arrived at the construction camp, around thirty people were there, most of them operating huge machines that ate up big chucks of dirt and moved boulders as if they were toy building blocks. She was pleased to see a woman driving one of the behemoths and another, obviously in the last trimester of pregnancy, going into a trailer that had a sign declaring it to be the office.

Jeremy led the way to it. "Tina Ramsey, Zia Peters," he introduced her to the pregnant woman. "Tina is the executive assistant of the site and keeps things on track around here. Zia is the new curriculum coordinator for the county education department. She arrived in town yesterday."

"Glad to meet you," the younger woman said. "Are you at the residential hotel? Everyone stays there when they arrive."

"Yes. I rented a suite for a month while I'm looking for a place of my own," Zia told the friendly younger woman.

"My cousin Jim is in real estate. You should check with him. Are you looking to rent or buy?"

"Rent for now. I would like a small house, if possible."

Tina wrinkled her nose. "Those are hard to find. People tend to stay put." Her laughter was infectious. "There was an article in the local paper about the county's plans for the school system, if the federal funds come through. It mentioned you."

Zia liked the vivacious young woman. She was friendly and very pretty with thick black hair that almost reached her waist, fair skin and intriguing gray eyes that flashed like quicksilver as she talked.

Tina turned her attention to her boss. "I have the lading bills for you to look over. Also, I need your signature for the overtime hours last week."

Zia glanced out the trailer window at the busy

compound while they conferred. Jeremy had just started his new position, yet the two seemed very comfortable with each other.

She wasn't particularly comfortable with anyone at first meeting. For her, friendship had to grow slowly. Only time would tell if the person was trustworthy. Her attitude was a lot different from what it had been at one time, when she'd been prone to snap judgments.

Maybe part of turning over a new leaf was learning to trust others without so many of the reservations learned from the past.

"Come on," Jeremy said. "I'll show you around."

Jeremy, like his uncle, was one of the most honorable people she'd ever met, she mused as she fell into step beside him. He would never walk out on anyone who needed him....

He took her arm and led the way outside, interrupting the unsettling introspection.

The gorge where the new road would cross was narrow and deep. Below them, the river rushed over rocks as big as cars. The land on either side was beautiful in a wild, natural way that didn't invite habitation.

"This will be the foundation of a rainbow bridge," Jeremy explained, pointing out the concrete piers.

"Rainbow?" That sounded too fanciful for a bridge.

"The roadbed will be built across the top of an arch made of steel beams and attached to piers on each side. It's a fairly simple form of construction and very strong. The Chinese used the technique a couple of thousand years ago, only they built the whole bridge from logs lashed together and the arch also functioned as the road. Unfortunately none are standing now, we only have a few engravings to go by."

By the time they'd finished the tour, including crossing to the other side and back on a rather precarious—in her opinion—footbridge, she'd learned a lot more about bridges than was strictly necessary in her view. She was aware of amusement in Jeremy's eyes as he gave her the guided tour.

The footbridge was like a ladder laid across the gorge with flimsy ropes for railings. The workers could probably dash across as sure-footed as the bighorn they'd seen earlier.

Zia kept her eyes on where she put her feet, aware of the water ten stories below and of the gaps between the foot supports which looked wide enough to fall through.

"You handled that very well," Jeremy commented when they had safely returned to the main camp. "Some people can't take seeing the empty space below them. They freeze."

"It wasn't empty," she muttered dryly. "There was a river moving at around sixty miles an hour a hundred feet below."

That caused the workers who overheard them to laugh with far more enthusiasm than the remark deserved. Jeremy joined in.

She managed a weak smile and shook her head.

"It's almost noon," he said. "Ready for lunch?"

"Here?"

He nodded. "We have a mess tent."

"I hope it's on this side of the river." She grinned as everyone again laughed and went with Jeremy to a metal-roofed building with canvas sides behind the office trailer. "Wow, air-conditioning."

He explained the luxury to her. "It gets so hot in the summer, the workers need a break from the heat at times."

The temperature was in the eighties now, but in July and August, the thermometer would climb into the mid-nineties on average during the day. At night, it could drop to around fifty, or even into the forties. Although usually dry during the summer, thunderstorms could bring flash floods. The high desert was not a place for careless people.

They went through a buffet line that offered several entrées of meat and vegetables, then sat at a long table where Tina and two women were already seated. Zia recognized one of them as the equipment operator she'd noticed when they first arrived. Jeremy introduced the three. "Paula and Marti, this is Zia."

"How did you learn to handle that huge machine?" Zia asked Marti after they said hello.

"School," Marti told her. "At heavy equipment schools, you learn to handle all kinds of machines. My dad had a road repair company, but he wouldn't let me work for him. So I decided to show him women could handle dozers the same as men."

"She's one of the best," Jeremy added. "She agreed to come here from the Salt Lake area after I showed her the article on the new education plans. In a way, you helped me hire her."

"I have a boy and girl, sixth and fourth grades," the woman continued the story. "I wasn't sure the schools were as good here as in the city."

"The curriculum planning is part of a new federal program being tried in several states. I'm excited about it," Zia said.

She and Marti, who looked around forty, discussed the school situation in depth during most of the meal. Once when she glanced at Jeremy, he had a thoughtful smile on his handsome face as he observed them. She smiled back and returned to the conversation.

He, his assistant and the other woman, who kept up with expenses for the DOT, held their own discussion of site problems while they ate. Zia listened after the equipment operator left to go back to work.

Apparently cost was a big factor in Jeremy's being moved from his former work site near Bryce Canyon to Uinta County. The bridge construction was way past schedule and over budget. He was to get things moving and under control.

Listening to him, she felt a totally unwarranted sense of pride at his masterful grasp of the situation. It was obvious the other two respected his decisions. She was glad things were working out so well for him in his new position.

Shortly after one, they were on the road again, heading north toward town. "Was that any fun for you at all?" he asked.

"Oh, yes. I enjoyed it a lot. The scenery was great, as promised, and the building site was very interesting. I feel like an expert on road construction now and will amaze my friends when I explain rainbow bridges to them."

He laughed heartily at her claim, which pleased her.

As they passed the city limits sign, she became somber. She *had* enjoyed herself, perhaps too much. She couldn't rely on Jeremy for companionship. It wouldn't be fair. His time would be better spent finding the woman of his dreams.

Her mother had indicated she was worried about Jeremy and the fact that he'd never married. Caileen thought it was because of the unsettled life he'd lived during his youth. His father had died of a heart attack at a very young age, then his uncle—the middle Aquilon brother—rolled his truck one snowy night and died of exposure before being found. The problems with Family Services before being left in peace with his uncle Jeff had probably made him as cautious in love as her experience with Sammy had made her.

Besides, she didn't think Jeremy liked her very much. She'd known, from the moment they'd first met, that he thought of her as a willful only child who'd given her mom grief for no good reason, not like Krista and Tony being beaten by a foster father or having a father drop dead like Jeremy. By contrast she'd had an easy life.

She'd just taken it hard, she admitted sardonically.

"You don't have to pretend with me, you know," he continued as they neared the hotel, his manner thoughtful.

She was astounded. "I'm not acting, Jeremy. I really did have a great time today. I liked the tour. It was interesting talking to your workers." She paused. "I was tired last night, so I probably wasn't very good company. I'm sorry if I disappointed you in some way."

"I didn't mean to give that impression. But, it occurs to me that you might have felt pressured to, uh, be friendly. I want you to know you don't have to. We don't have to see each other at all."

She laid her head back on the seat and laughed softly. "We're both fools," she told him. "I thought you were being nice because you felt you had to take care of me. I can't believe Mom called and asked you to check that I arrived safely. As if I were a ten-year-old off on my first trip alone. Honestly," she ended in amused exasperation.

"Okay, I guess we understand each other then," he said. "No more Mr. Nice Guy," he added in the tough manner of an action-adventure hero.

"Right. We can check in on each other once in a while to keep the folks off our case, but otherwise we go our own ways."

"Agreed."

When he stopped at the hotel, she jumped down from the SUV before he could get out. "Thanks again for the tour. As soon as I find a place to live, I'll invite you to dinner."

He gave her a calculating glance. "A home-cooked meal would be nice, like the meat loaf your mom makes."

"Can do," she assured him. "I'll get in touch when I'm settled. Okay?"

After he nodded, she closed the truck door and headed for her room. Standing on the porch, she watched him drive down the street. It made her feel good to be on solid footing with him, she realized. Maybe they *could* be friends.

Casual friends, she amended, going into her pleasant room. Occasional friends, the type you talk to whenever you run into each other on the street. Maybe they would have coffee once in a while, or lunch. Nothing that demanded a lot of fuss and bother, or that could be called a relationship.

Anything more would never work between them. The past would always be there, ready to spring up when least expected, reminding her of the reasons she didn't want any connection to her misguided youth. He would probably prefer to avoid her, too.

However, when she'd danced with him at the wedding, she hadn't been thinking of the past at all. Instead, her foolish heart had envisioned a future filled with all the good things that could exist between a couple who truly loved each other.

The intense longing returned. She wanted...she wanted something different from life. Maybe she would find it here.

She sighed as she settled into a chair and stared out the window at the sweeping vista of mountains. She would keep her word and invite Jeremy to dinner when she found a home, then...then her obligation to him would be done.

Chapter Three

Zia shook hands with the real estate agent. "Thanks for your help. If I see anything that looks interesting this weekend, I'll call you on Monday."

"Same here," Jim Ramsey said.

She had contacted Tina Ramsey's cousin on Monday. Jim was around her age, about two inches shorter and heavyset. He was outgoing and cheerful, also enthusiastic about her finding a place to live.

But after searching all week—today was Friday—the prospects didn't look great, in her opinion.

"There are places coming on the market all the time," he assured her in a hearty manner. "If you want to buy, I know of several cottages for sale, a couple of them in town or close in, more in the country."

"I'll think about it."

"Sure you don't want a ride to the hotel?"

She shook her head. "I'll walk. I like the exercise."

She strolled down the street, leaving him in front of the real estate office, which was two blocks from the educational building. One thing about a small town— one was never far from anywhere in it.

When she passed the DOT facility, she quickly scanned the parking lot. She spotted Jeremy's SUV near the side entrance.

"Hey," he called to her, coming out the door at that moment.

His appearance startled her as it had last Friday when she'd arrived in town, as if an apparition had suddenly materialized.

"Jeremy, hello," she said, breathless for no reason...no reason at all. He was dressed in dark slacks and a white shirt with a tie. A suit jacket was slung over his shoulder. With his summer Stetson, he looked, she thought, like a rugged Western hero on a photo shoot for some classy magazine.

He came over to the sidewalk. "How's it going?"

"If you're talking about the house search, it isn't." She managed a smile so he wouldn't think she was whining.

"What's the problem?"

"I'm not sure," she said ruefully, "but I think my finances don't match my tastes."

When he laughed, his teeth were incredibly white against the tawny shades of his skin. He had a killer smile. It highlighted his whole face, forcing her to realize anew his natural good looks and masculine grace, both of which were reasons why her friends had always wanted to get acquainted with him.

"Have you had lunch?" he asked. "I'm going now and would be glad to have company."

She hesitated, then nodded. "I just got back from house hunting with Jim Ramsey."

"Tina's cousin? I seem to recall her mentioning him."

"She did. He seems to know the area really well. We've been over on the east side of town, out in the county, actually."

"My place is out that way, too." Jeremy took her arm and guided her down the street. He pointed out two restaurants. "Mexican or the soup and sandwich place?"

"Mexican," she decided. "I ate at the sandwich place yesterday. The food was delicious. The owner there was the one who told me to check out the cottages east of town. She said people were selling their vacation homes or renting them since prices had started falling."

After they were inside the restaurant and sipping from tall, frosty glasses of iced tea, they quickly made their selections and ordered.

"I like a woman who can make up her mind," he said when they were alone again.

She had to smile at his rueful tone. "Is that something you've had a problem with in the past?"

"Just once. When I was stationed in Salt Lake City for six months, I dated a woman who managed a gift shop. I don't know how she ever ordered merchandise because it took her a week to decide what she wanted for dinner."

"Mmm, you must have had very long dates."

He gave her a wry grimace. "Okay, maybe it only took her thirty minutes, but it seemed like a week."

Their salads arrived, and they ate in silence for a few minutes. Zia tried to think of something to say, but her mind stayed stubbornly on the woman who had lost out on a relationship with him. "I assume you didn't ask her out again?"

"Actually I did, but it was the same the second time. When she invited me to a cookout with friends, I had to decline because I'd been transferred to the Bryce Canyon project."

"You were glad," Zia said in slightly accusatory tones.

"I was. The move made it easier to break it off."

She eyed him thoughtfully. "I think men still have the advantage in dating, especially if you made the first contact. You can simply not call again."

"What if she calls you?"

"Screen your calls and let the answering machine pick up if you don't want to talk."

"And don't call back?"

"Right. That's what my friends do with a guy they don't want to see again. Wouldn't the same tactic work for men?"

"I suppose."

"What?" she said when he frowned.

"It doesn't seem quite fair to leave someone dangling."

"So what do you do if you haven't been transferred

to a new location and you don't want to see someone again?" she asked, then was annoyed at herself for the blatant curiosity about him and his dating life.

"I tell them that work is going to keep me busy for several weeks. Which is mostly true," he added. "And I'm out of town at the construction sites a lot, too."

"I have a friend who studied ethics. She said the truth told in an untruthful way is still a lie." Zia grinned as she waited to see what he would say to that.

"What about you?" he asked, giving her a narrow-eyed scrutiny and ignoring her gibe. "What do you do to fend off unwanted men? You must get calls by the score."

"Hardly. I don't usually accept dates unless I've known the man for a while." When he raised his eyebrows at this, she continued, "I like to get to know people and see how they respond in social situations before being alone with them. It makes things easier, don't you think?"

"Yes," he said softly, "I do."

Something in his eyes made her wonder if she'd said too much. Being cautious was probably not the way he thought of her. She'd once acted rashly, impulsively and the consequences be damned.

"Well, back to the housing market," she said brightly. "Do you have any advice? Should I think about buying?"

"How do you feel about your job?" he asked.

She was surprised. "Well, I don't really know. I talked to the superintendent of schools on Monday, looked my office over on Tuesday and met the department secretary on Wednesday. She looks as if she moved in when the facility was built. I have no idea if I'll last longer than my three-year contract."

"You got a contract?"

"Yes. It's an administrative position. Instead of tenure, we agree on a specified time to put my ideas into action and see results." She shrugged. "If things don't turn around as fast as the school board thinks it should, they have to buy out the contract to get rid of me."

"Mmm, maybe you'd better wait before buying a house, at least until you have a few months under your belt."

"That's what I thought, too." She sighed. "Finding a small house to rent is more difficult than I thought it would be."

"That's why I bought a place. I thought I'd be here for at least ten years, but then we ran into problems in the southwest region again. I've used a lot of vacation time to work on the cabin, though. It's coming along. I'll get a lot more done now that I'm stationed here."

"How long do you think you'll be in this district?"

"I plan to retire here." His charming grin popped up. "Unless they want to put me in charge of the whole DOT. I don't see that happening."

"Why not?"

"There's too much politics going on at the state level. I'd tell some big shot where to get off and probably be out the door in record time."

"I've always found you to be very tactful," she assured him.

He was silent for a minute, then his eyes met hers. "With some people, it's easier to be gentle than with others."

Gentle.

The word lingered in Zia's mind at the grocery where she bought fruit, bread and peanut butter and at the Laundromat where she washed and dried the clothing she'd worn that week.

Later, as evening painted the sky in soft hues, she sat on the side porch of the hotel and ate a solitary meal, the word echoing in her head like thunder reverberating off distant mountain peaks, plangent and haunting.

Jeremy was referring to women, she decided. Actually he was gentle with all who were smaller, weaker than himself. Look how wonderful he'd been with his stepcousins, rescuing Tony and Krista from that horrible foster father when they were children. Both had grown up to be fine, decent citizens, thanks to his influence as well as his uncle's.

Whoever caught his heart would be loved and cherished forever. A lucky woman.

She tried to put the luncheon conversation out of mind, but words and phrases kept popping up like new bits of scenery with each curve in a winding road.

She suddenly wished Jeremy was with her. She wanted to ask him about…about life and love and what it all meant…

"Miss Peters?"

She jerked at the sound of her name. A young man

stood at the corner of the porch. The night clerk, she realized.

"Yes, that's me."

"You have a call. Shall I transfer it to your room phone?"

"Yes, please. Thank you," she added, hurrying inside.

A second later, the phone rang. She sat on the bed and picked up the receiver. "Hello?"

"Zia?"

"Yes. Who's this?"

"Heather. I tried to get you on your cell phone but couldn't get an answer."

"It's on the charger," Zia explained, her mind racing.

Heather. Her mother's longtime friend. There was only one reason she would be calling.

"What's happened?" Zia asked, steeling herself for bad news.

"Your mother is ill. An infection of some kind. The ambulance is taking her to the hospital in Boise. Jeff is with her. He asked me to call."

"An infection?" Zia questioned. "Where?"

"It's in her gall bladder and liver. Apparently it caused the bile duct to close and destroy most of her liver before they realized what the problem was."

Zia tried to take in the information, but a sense of panic was setting in fast. "What are they going to do at the Boise hospital?" The city was an hour away, and there was a small county hospital in their hometown.

Heather hesitated before saying, "Stop the infection, first of all. There's internal bleeding. They'll have to take care of that, too. The liver damage is pretty serious. I, uh, I think you'd better consider coming home."

Zia had already determined that. "I'll be there by morning," she said. "Have you called anyone else?"

"No, you're the first one who came to mind. Do you want me to call your dad?"

"I—I don't know. No. I'll call him tomorrow...when we know more." She pressed a hand to her forehead. "Jeremy. I can contact him. We need to call Tony and Julianne. Krista and Lance are still on their honeymoon. They're someplace in Europe. Let's wait on them."

"Right. Jeff gave me Caileen's address book. That's where I got your cell number. When I didn't get an answer, I remembered you were staying at the hotel. Caileen had mentioned the name at lunch the other day."

Heather, a paralegal from juvenile court, and her mother had been having lunch once a week for as long as Zia could remember.

"When I called the hotel, the clerk said he'd seen you outside when he came on duty," Heather finished.

"Thank God," Zia murmured. "I'll call Jeremy and start packing. Is there anything else I need to do?"

"Not that I can think of. I'll call your cell number if anything changes. Jeff asked if I could be the message hub in case you guys have trouble getting through at the hospital."

"Thanks, Heather. I'll be there as soon as possible."

"Drive carefully. We don't need you in an accident."

"Yes, I'll be careful."

After hanging up, Zia clicked on Jeremy's number,

but either his cell phone was off or he was out of range. She left a voice mail for him to call her right away. Then she grabbed her largest case and tossed the contents of the bureau into it, mostly jeans, T-shirts and underwear. Since her overnight case held her makeup and toiletries, she closed it and set it next to the larger piece.

In less than fifteen minutes, with jacket and purse in hand, she was ready to go. Dusk had deepened to twilight as she tried Jeremy again.

Still no answer.

After putting her luggage in her car, she went to the hotel desk and explained to the night clerk about the family emergency and left her cell number with him in case anyone needed to get in touch.

"You're keeping your room?" he asked.

"Yes. I still have some things in it."

"Very good. Be careful on the road. People drive too fast since there's not much traffic."

"Thanks, I will."

After trying Jeremy once more, she located his address on the county map and headed out. It didn't occur to her until she was well on her way that he might not consider it necessary to go to Idaho. He might prefer to wait until they knew the situation.

Whatever his decision, she was definitely going home.

She found his mailbox on the county road, the numbers reflecting in her headlights so they were easy to read. She turned onto the gravel drive.

In a couple of minutes she came upon the house tucked into a clearing among the pines and cedars. It wasn't the rustic cabin she'd expected. Instead it looked more like a small, elegant lodge with stones in desert hues of ocher and terra-cotta covering the bottom half and a very soft terra-cotta stucco on the upper part. A window in the gable indicated an attic room under the eaves.

His SUV was under the attached carport, and a light was on inside. Relieved, she parked and hurried to the door.

The oak door was open, but a screen door kept out intruders. Hearing footsteps, she leaned close and peered in.

"Jeremy?" she called upon spotting movement in the dim hall.

The figure paused. "Zia?"

"Yes." Without waiting for an invitation, she opened the screen door and went inside. "I'm so glad you're home—"

That's when it hit her that he'd just come out of the shower. In the soft light of the living room lamp, she caught only an impression of a muscular male body before he disappeared.

She went totally still for a second. "I'm sorry," she called out, impatient with the unexpected rise in temperature and heartbeat his naked presence engendered. This was no time for niceties. "I didn't mean to barge in, but there's an emergency."

He stepped back into view, a towel secured around his lean hips. "What kind of emergency?"

"My mother is very ill. Jeff is taking her to Boise in an ambulance."

"What's wrong?"

She told him what she knew.

He nodded, then brushed the lock of damp hair off his forehead. "That sounds serious," he said, taking a couple of steps into the room.

"I'm on my way to the hospital. I thought, if you wanted to go, we could travel together. Mom…" Her throat closed up.

"Are you packed and ready?"

She nodded.

"Give me ten minutes."

He disappeared into another room farther down the hall. She sank into a deep leather chair that faced the hearth. Her heart steadied. She exhaled a somewhat shaky breath and gazed around the room. The walls had a plaster finish, Tuscan-style, with pale golden paint glazed with sienna. It was very attractive.

The kitchen was small and tucked into an alcove behind the right-hand side of the great room. The cabinets were cedar, the appliances new and modern. An island with a cooktop separated it from the living area, which spanned the width of the house. The sofa was rich, brown leather that matched the chair she sat in. Another chair, also a recliner, was smaller and upholstered in a deep terra-cotta and tan chenille.

A long hassock with a tray on it served as a coffee table. Attractive floor lamps anchored each end of the sofa. A low chest of drawers with two buffet lamps nestled under a side window that framed a view of woods and a creek.

A round table of oak with six chairs and a breakfront cabinet occupied the other end of the broad living space.

She wondered who had picked out the furnishings. A woman, she concluded. She couldn't imagine Jeremy giving much thought to interior design.

He returned to the living room and tossed a duffel bag on the floor near the door. A shaving kit landed beside it.

"I need a few more minutes," he said, going into the kitchen.

Opening a cedar-lined door, which proved to be the refrigerator, he removed several items. He poured the milk down the drain, ran some leftovers through the disposal and tossed salad greens far out the side door.

"There, that should do it," he said with another glance around the neat space.

"Your home is very nice," she said, rising.

He smiled, but it didn't erase the worried look in his eyes. "Someday I'll show you the pictures I took before I started the remodel. The place didn't have a lot going for it."

"Did you pick out the furniture?"

"Yeah, but Krista advised me on colors and all that. I sent her pictures by phone and she okayed the sofa and chairs. The couple who own the furniture store did the layout and talked me into that chest. I think they called it a credenza."

"The hassock and tray are very up-to-date."

"It's also great to prop your feet on when the guys are over for beer and pizza night."

She managed a laugh.

He came around the island and laid a hand on her shoulder. "It'll be okay. Caileen is tough. She'll make it."

She nodded, unable to speak for a second. "Are you ready?"

"Yes. I'll call a couple of my supervisors when we get to town and put them in charge until I get back."

"We probably won't be gone long." The words sounded false even to her ears.

"Let's hit the road." He waited for her to exit, then turned out the lights and locked up. "We'll use the SUV."

She didn't argue, but went to her car and got her luggage while he stored his in the back of his vehicle. He added her two cases when she brought them over.

"Do you want to leave your car here or in town?"

"Is it okay here?"

He nodded. "I've never had any trouble."

"I'll leave it."

After ushering her into the passenger seat, he belted himself in and they left on a journey that would take them most of the night. "Maybe we won't have any road delays at night," she said as he turned onto the paved county road.

"Yeah, that'll be a real plus."

In town, he stopped by the DOT office and called those who needed to know where he was going while she waited in the SUV. When he returned, he had a large insulated container of coffee and two plastic cups, plus two cans of soda. He placed a small wire basket of snacks—peanuts, crackers, chips, two apples—on the center console.

"This should get us through until breakfast," he told her, heading west on the highway out of town.

"It took me several hours to make the trip home for

Krista's wedding," she murmured, gazing past the sweep of the headlights into the countryside when they were west of town.

Glancing at his profile, she recalled how handsome, how…how cosmopolitan he'd seemed at the wedding. She'd thought of Jeremy as an earthy sort—well, being a civil engineer, that seemed natural—but she'd discovered another side to him, one that was urbane and at ease in the most elegant surroundings.

Pulling her gaze back to the countryside, she frowned at the sudden pang that went through her, a piercing moment of longing for something that was missing in her life, that had always been just beyond her grasp. She couldn't say what it was.

The moon limned the pavement into a ghostly ribbon. She saw no lights ahead to indicate oncoming traffic. They could have been the only creatures in the world. It was an eerie sensation.

Jeremy set the cruise control, popped the top on one of the cans and took a long drink, then placed it in a cup holder. "I haven't had dinner," he said as he tore open a bag of chips with his teeth.

"Oh, I'm sorry. I'd eaten earlier. I didn't think about your missing dinner," she finished.

"That's okay. I'd just gotten in from the bridge site shortly before you arrived. I decided I needed a bath more than food at the moment."

"Are you having problems with the construction?"

"Yes. There's soft rock layered in with the hard stuff. We have to have a solid base for the piers."

"So what will you do?"

"Drill pilings through the soft rock. It'll cost more and delay the construction. Again."

"That's too bad."

"The department won't be too happy about it, but, as I always say—live with it."

She found herself smiling at his sardonic amusement in spite of her worry. Talking helped pass the time, she found. "I've never heard you say that. I've never seen you as a cynic."

"Stick around," he advised, "and you'll discover the real me. It isn't a pretty picture."

Her laughter was brief, a little shaky, but real. The moment seemed lighter, the night not so dark.

The moon rose higher over the mesas, brightening the landscape. Deep blue shadows cast strange shapes over the sandy soil around huge boulders. Sagebrush, with its golden blooms, looked like squat watchers of the night as the truck sped by.

An average of three trucks an hour passed them, heading east toward Vernal, bringing groceries and goods to the town. They met one other passenger car near the town, then none until they closed in on Salt Lake City. The interstate highway had lots more traffic, but it zoomed along rapidly.

"He must have been doing eighty," she murmured when a sporty-looking vehicle zipped by them.

"The road is pretty straight, so people tend to speed."

"Including you?"

"I'm conservative. I only go about five miles over the

limit," he said. "Would you pour me a cup of coffee? I'm going to need the caffeine from here on in. It's past my bedtime."

"Mine, too."

She saw him glance at her in the dim glow of the dash lights. "Odd, but I really don't know much about you, whether you're a day or night person, if you wake up grouchy or in a good mood."

She handed him the steaming cup. "Careful," she warned, settling back in the seat once he held the cup. "Basically, you know everything about me. You know both my parents. You know about my early life, the asthma I outgrew, the schools I went to. You went to them, too, all except for my last years at the university in Oregon when I worked for my father and shared an apartment with his foreman's daughter."

"Did you like living there?"

"It was okay. I'd learned a lot by then, so I wasn't…I wasn't like I was with my mother," she admitted with a break in her voice. "I've always wanted to apologize for giving her such a hard time. I may never have the chance," she ended dismally.

"She'll be fine," he said, understanding the direction of her thoughts. "Why don't you call and see what's happening? Heather may have some news."

"That's a good idea." Zia pulled up Heather's number on her phone. In a moment, her mom's best friend answered. "Heather? It's Zia. Jeremy and I are on the road, past Salt Lake City on the interstate. Have you heard anything?"

"Yes. Jeff called. Caileen is in surgery. He says she's holding up fine and was in good spirits when they took her into the OR," she ended on an encouraging note.

"That sounds great. I'll call again when we get closer to Boise. Let me know if anything changes."

"I will."

"Thanks for everything. We should be in around dawn." After hanging up, she reported the info to Jeremy.

"It sounds as if they have everything under control."

They were silent for a few minutes, each lost in thought. She sighed. "I think I'll try to sleep. When you want me to drive, just say so."

"I'll let you take over when we stop for gas. That'll be in another hour or so."

"Okay." She let the seat back as far as it would go and pulled her jacket across her shoulders. The night air continued to cool down as they rushed across the desert. Inside, she felt the chill of dread and worry that she couldn't suppress.

Jeremy reached over and tucked the jacket more securely around her. His hand brushed her chin and sent a surge of warmth down her neck. It lodged in her heart and from there radiated out to her whole body. It was the oddest sensation.

"Thanks," she whispered.

She was glad to have him with her. It was good to have someone to share the worry, she mused sleepily.

She hadn't let herself rely on anyone, including her parents, since starting her career. She'd made it a rule not to bother others with her problems, whatever they were.

But with Jeremy, it was different. He was dependable, she thought as she drifted into sleep. He cared about her mom, too, so his concern was real.

It wasn't until she'd been in trouble and unable, due to pride, shame and a whole bunch of other emotions, to go to her parents that she'd realized how important they were to her. It wasn't until she was living with her father that she'd realized how much she missed her mother. It wasn't until she was desperate that she'd realized how desperate her mother must have been at times, with no one to call on for help.

Jeremy had come to *her* when she'd needed someone. Just as he was here now, sharing the burden with her. She wasn't going to lean on him, but it was comforting, knowing she could and that she could go to sleep and he would still be there, calm and steady, when she awoke.

Chapter Four

Zia woke to the sound of her name. She sat up and looked around, groggy and disoriented. She realized Jeremy was off the highway and entering the parking lot of a service station. There were several big rigs lined up along one side of the brightly lit place, but only one other passenger vehicle.

"What time is it?" she asked.

"Nearly four."

She glanced at the eastern sky. The soft gray of morning brightened the horizon. "You let me sleep," she accused.

"You didn't wake up when I stopped for gas, and I felt okay, so I continued."

"Where are we?"

"Near Boise. You ready for breakfast? I thought we could eat now, then go straight to the hospital when we get in."

She nodded, then stretched and yawned. "I feel like I'm in a time warp or something. Everything seems strange."

"Traveling at night, then waking in a different place makes you feel off-kilter." He looked her over. "They have showers here. I think I'll take one before we eat. How about you?"

"That's a good idea. Maybe it'll clear my foggy brain," she murmured with a feeble attempt at humor.

He smiled. "If not, the coffee will. I've stopped here before. The house blend is strong enough to dissolve metal."

Taking a change of clothing with them, they each had a shower and freshened up. Zia admitted she did feel much better when she met Jeremy at the restaurant entrance.

After eating from the breakfast buffet, they headed out again, the insulated container filled with fresh coffee.

"Heather's cell number is on my phone," she said when they were on the highway with her behind the wheel. "Do you think we should call and see how things are?"

"The sun isn't up yet. She might be asleep."

"Right."

He touched her shoulder briefly, then withdrew. "She or Uncle Jeff will call if things change."

"Yes, you're right."

He found a news station on the radio. They listened to the weather, which was predicted to be fair and sunny with temperatures in the low eighties. Zia felt there should be dark clouds hovering over the truck as they sped along the highway.

That was the way she felt inside.

She glanced at Jeremy. The twin furrows of a frown cut lines across his forehead. His normal expression was one of serious concentration, she'd noticed on more than one occasion, but now there was the added intensity of worry. It haunted his eyes and reflected the apprehension she, too, felt.

As they neared Boise, the traffic increased, but there were no slowdowns, thanks to the early hour. Jeremy tried Caileen's cell phone, in hopes that his uncle had it with him, but got no response. Zia turned off the interstate. A few minutes later, as dawn spilled over the horizon, she pulled into the parking lot of the hospital and stopped.

"We're here," she murmured, almost reluctant to go inside.

"We'll see how things are," Jeremy said. "Then I'll check on donating blood. It's been over two months for me, so they can take another pint."

Zia was reminded of the time he and Jeff had both come to the hospital in Council, where she and her mom had lived at the time, to donate blood for her. "That's a good idea. I'll do the same. Mom and I are both A-positive."

Inside, Jeremy asked directions at the reception desk, then they went up to the third floor and followed the signs to the intensive care wing. His uncle Jeff stood at the door of the waiting room.

The three of them exchanged quick, comforting embraces.

"Caileen is in the IC room now," he told them, the lines in his face deeper than usual. "She came through the surgery just fine. They got the bleeding stopped and the antibiotics seem to be working on the infection. The surgeon stopped by. She told me Caileen would be kept in a light coma while her body repairs itself. The doctors want her to be very still and to put as little demand on her internal organs as possible."

"Can we see her?" Zia asked.

"You'll have to ask the nurse," Jeff said. "I just came from there and we're only allowed in for five minutes each hour."

Jeremy had always seen his uncle as strong and invincible, a child's view, he now realized, observing the fatigue in every line of the other man's body, the depth of worry in his eyes.

"What happened?" he asked. "How did the infection get started?"

"A small gallstone partially blocked the duct." Jeff ran a hand around the back of his neck, massaging the tight muscles. "That eventually caused a complete blockage. Bile backed up into the liver, nearly destroying it before we realized what was wrong. The infection started after that."

Jeremy nodded. "Have you had any sleep?"

"Not yet," his uncle admitted.

"There's no one in the waiting room," Zia said, laying a hand on the older man's arm. "And there's nothing to do but wait. Why don't you rest while you can? We'll wake you if anything changes."

Jeremy was somewhat surprised at the insightful suggestion.

"Maybe I will," Jeff agreed. "Go through the ICU doors and check in with the nurse. Caileen is in room B1."

Inside, the nurses' station was located in the center of the area with patients' rooms opening off three sides of the encircling hallway. "Caileen Aquilon?" Jeremy said to the young woman who glanced up at them.

"Are you relatives?"

"Her daughter," Zia spoke up. She glanced at Jeff. "And her nephew."

The nurse checked Caileen's record. "She's still unconscious, but she may be able to hear your voice. Speak softly and calmly. Even when patients don't visibly react, they often respond to a loved one's presence." She gave them a smile. "Room B1. Five minutes. But I don't check the clock very often," she added with a kind smile.

Jeremy ushered Zia into the room. Caileen lay totally still in the bed, her skin as pale as the sheets. A ventilator, which no one had mentioned, made a whooshing sound as it helped her breathe. Tubes were everywhere, it seemed, and monitors reported on her vital functions.

Zia's gasp revealed her reaction.

He laid an arm around her shoulders. "She's resting," he said, trying to be reassuring.

Zia turned her face and pressed it to his shoulder. "Dear God," she whispered, so low he barely caught the words.

After a minute, when she once again stared at her mother, he spoke quietly, "Hey, Caileen. It's Zia and Jeremy. We drove up last night and just got in. We talked to Uncle Jeff. He's resting on the waiting room sofa."

Zia started when he ran out of words. "I really like the residential hotel where I'm staying in Vernal. Everyone is very nice and they serve a delicious high tea from five until seven. I usually have soup for dinner at a great restaurant in town, then have dessert at the hotel. The scones are delicious."

"She hasn't invited me over to share in the bounty," Jeremy said in a mock-aggrieved tone. "And I took her to the best steak house in town, too. That's gratitude for you."

"Hey, I was grateful," Zia said. "I just didn't show it…my usual gracious manner," she added.

They both made sounds that could have passed for laughter.

Caileen, a person he loved almost as much as his uncle, didn't move a muscle. In the quiet, the only sound was the airy swish of the ventilator. He saw Zia's gaze on it, her expression one of ravaged sorrow.

That was more emotion than he'd ever seen in her, and it surprised him. Okay, so maybe she was capable of deeper feelings than he'd credited her with. But after all, he added, that was her mother lying there looking like death warmed over.

"Our five minutes are up," he murmured.

"I want to stay a while longer."

He nodded and, without thinking, kissed her on the temple. "She's strong," he said. "Like you."

Zia gave him a slight smile, then turned back to the bed. He went down to check on his uncle.

Zia sat on the one chair in the room and stared at the still form, the sound of the ventilator regulating her own breathing to its rhythm. Her mother was strong, just as Jeremy said.

But not me, she admitted. He was wrong about that. She was filled with dread, as if something in her already knew the outcome and that it wasn't good. Had she ever told Caileen how much she loved her, how much she appreciated the sacrifices her mom had made to provide a good home for her?

As the familiar regret filled her, she chided herself for being selfish. Wanting forgiveness for her past sins was about her. Right now, the patient needed all her hopes and prayers.

Stifling a fierce stab of despair, she laid a hand over the still one on the sheet. The flesh was cool and seemed fragile, so very fragile....

This hand had soothed her cuts and bruises so many times. Those pale lips had kissed her hurts and made them better. She longed to do the same for the parent who had always been there, who had put her child's life and health above her own desires, even her marriage.

"Mom," she whispered. "I'm here for you. Jeff and Jeremy are, too. Please don't let go."

For a second, there was only the sound of her

quickly drawn breath and the compression of the breathing machine, then she felt the faintest movement against her hand.

Had her mom tried to squeeze her hand? Or was it only her own wishful thinking that made her feel something that wasn't there?

"I felt that," she said, trying to sound upbeat. "I felt your hand move in mine. That was good. Very good."

She tried to think of funny things to say, cheerful incidents that would remind them of happier times.

"Remember that time we tried to make ice cream with that old freezer a neighbor threw out? I dragged the rusty thing home and you worked and worked on it until the gears came unstuck, but the cleanser didn't all wash out and got into the ice cream so then we were afraid to eat it. I was so disappointed. We went out for a banana split instead. You used our grocery money, so we ate peanut butter sandwiches every day the next week."

Zia paused and smiled at the memory as a mist formed in her eyes. She blinked it away.

"I've always loved peanut butter sandwiches since then," she said, her voice going shaky as her throat tightened. "Comfort food. That's what you would call it."

The hot press of tears caused her to grit her teeth. Picking up her purse, she left the room, determined not to cry. Her mom didn't need that.

Going down the corridor and through the swinging doors, she joined Jeremy in the waiting room. Jeff was asleep on the sofa.

"I think we should call the rest of the family," she whispered. "Don't you?"

He nodded, then glanced at his uncle as he stirred restlessly. "Let's go down the hall."

In the corridor next to the elevators, they found a meditation room that was unoccupied. Unable to reach the traveling newlyweds, Zia sent a text message. Tony's cell phone was out of range. She called Tony's wife, a nurse-practitioner who headed up a clinic, and explained the situation.

"I've seen a similar case," Julianne told her. "The good news is, the liver is the only organ of the body that can regenerate itself if ten percent is still functional. There's a husband and wife team in San Francisco who have successfully transplanted part of one from a living donor and had it regenerate in both people."

After hanging up, she and Jeremy donated blood. The staff seemed particularly grateful for his O-negative pint. The technician, a very pretty woman around twenty-five, teased him about taking another pint.

"It's nice to be wanted," he quipped, lying on a table next to Zia.

No one teased her, she noted. It seemed a statement on her character. Was she totally unapproachable? She sighed, then felt a hand touch her arm. Her eyes met Jeremy's, and she was flooded with yearning so intense it hurt.

She managed a smile for him while she wondered about her emotional state of late. It wasn't just her mother's illness that bothered her, although that was enough in itself to give her gray hair. Lately, she seemed to overreact to every little thing.

Perhaps she just needed a change. Maybe that's why the new job had seemed so enticing. Change. She recalled from some class that the universe tended to chaos, that only precarious forces kept it all in order. She felt those forces were slipping badly where she was concerned.

"Okay," the perky technician said, "we're finished. Thanks for donating." She served them orange juice and made them sit for ten minutes before leaving the lab.

Once that was done, they returned to the waiting room and read magazines for three hours, stopping only to check on Caileen for five minutes out of every hour. Jeff slept as one exhausted. It occurred to her that he hadn't been able to rest until someone was available to take over the vigil for him.

Glancing at Jeremy, she saw he'd gone to sleep, too. His dark hair fell over his forehead with the same stubborn wave that Jeff had. Both men had the same lean, angular grace of movement that somehow spoke of confidence and the ability to handle whatever life threw at them.

They had always been kind to her, no matter what they may have thought of her actions when they first met. They had accepted her as if she really did belong....

A riot of emotion squeezed her heart like an invisible fist, and she was filled with gratitude and love, so much love, deep, aching and inexpressible, for all of them.

Why was that so hard to say?

* * *

"What time is it?"

Zia glanced at her watch as Jeremy sat up. Half the day had gone by. "A little past noon."

He rubbed his eyes, then went across the hall to the restroom. When he returned, he looked refreshed. The wave was combed back off his face. "There's a cafeteria here," he said. "You want to go down for lunch?"

She shook her head. "I'll stay in case the doctor comes by."

"You need to eat," Jeremy told her firmly. "It won't do anyone any good if you collapse."

His manner was light, but his eyes seemed to delve inside her and see her every thought.

"I think I could miss a meal or two without noticing it," she remarked wryly.

Jeff woke with a start, then stretched wearily. "Any news?"

"No change," Zia told him. "She's still sleeping."

"It's time for lunch," Jeremy told him. "Why don't you two check on Caileen? Let the nurse know we're going to the cafeteria and ask her to page us in case the doctor comes by."

"Good idea," Jeff agreed.

Zia went with Jeff into the intensive care wing. They stood silently by the bed and watched as Caileen's chest rose and fell in time to the ventilator.

"I've never seen her laid low," Zia said.

Jeff gave her a quick smile. "Neither have I. It's odd, isn't it, like there's another side to the person that you've never seen." He leaned over the bed. "Hey, girl," he murmured in a teasing manner. "Are you going to sleep all day? There're people here to see you."

As he talked softly, Zia heard tenderness in every word. She saw deep caring in his expression. There was a sense of expectation in him that Caileen would pull through, that she would fight the destruction in her body and make it.

True love. Zia may not have experienced it herself, but she knew it when she saw it. Gladness, like the soft light of dawn, stole over her. She was glad her mother had this man, this good, gentle man.

After the five minutes were up, she was subdued as the three of them walked down the steps to the first floor.

Seated around the cafeteria table, Jeff asked questions about their new location—the town and the country around it. Zia shared her recently acquired knowledge of bridge construction, bringing identical smiles to the men's faces at her description of the footbridge and her terror about crossing it.

They discussed the economy of the area and her chances of finding a cottage to fit her needs.

Jeremy spoke of the problems on road construction and the safety features of new highways. "It takes only a second of inattention and you can be in trouble," he told the other two. "That's one reason highway engineers like sound walls on each side of a major freeway. Tunnel vision keeps people focused on the road. Unless they're on their cell phones."

"We all go too fast," Zia said. "We rush through life."

She stopped as the others gave her sympathetic nods. She was aware of Jeremy's hand covering hers for a second.

His touch was…comforting.

It would be easy, she thought as they returned to the IC wing, to lean on him and his strength, to bask in the caring embrace of these two men. She wouldn't do that, but it was reassuring to know she could. If she really needed to.

The vigil continued. They checked on Caileen every hour. Jeremy made sure Zia and his uncle had coffee or walked down the stairs to the cafeteria for exercise and food. Otherwise they sat in the waiting room, sometimes sharing it with others who'd come to see their loved ones, but most times, alone.

Krista and Lance reported in as twilight blended into darkness. They were in Paris at a home appliance exhibition.

"She wants us to try every new idea she sees," Lance said.

Jeremy grinned at the tidbit of husbandly complaint. Krista liked to be in the middle of every project they tried, preferably as the boss. He wondered how the husband-and-wife team, both alpha types, managed to get anything done without killing each other.

The way all couples did, he decided. By talking things out and compromising, just the way Caileen insisted was necessary for civilized people to get along.

A knot formed in his throat, one made of love and memories and hope for the future.

Zia told Krista not to fly home immediately as the younger cousin wanted to do. "Let us find out what the doctor thinks first. I'll call as soon as he makes his rounds," she promised.

Tony also called when he returned to his and Julianne's home after a day at a new archaeological dig near Chaco Canyon. He wanted to know what they could do to help.

"Nothing at present," Jeremy advised. "We'll keep in touch."

At eight, Jeremy left, then returned to say he'd reserved adjoining rooms a block down the street at a bed-and-breakfast inn. He handed key cards to her and his uncle. "I thought we might need a place nearby to crash."

Jeff gave him a nod of gratitude. "Good thinking. I can stay here when they move Caileen from the ICU to a standard room. The nurse said the recliners can be made into beds."

At ten, Jeremy turned the TV on, and they listened to the news. A map showed the weather patterns across the country. A low system was heading their way, bringing rain and thunderclouds.

"Just what we need," Jeff said, for the first time sounding gloomy as well as worried.

A few minutes later, the three of them stood when a man dressed in a white jacket entered the waiting room. "Good evening. I'm Dr. Matherson."

"The ICU resident physician," Jeff told the other two as he shook hands with the doctor. "How is she?"

The doctor perched on the arm of a chair and indicated they should return to their seats. Jeremy moved over so Zia could sit on the sofa beside him. Her hip brushed his as she sat down, and fire flashed through him, making him acutely aware of her warmth and the lithe form that was so femininely attractive.

He took a deep breath and let it out slowly, annoyed with the physical reaction. When her eyes met his, his insides clenched and went on the alert as he realized she, too, was aware of the heat that flowed between them.

"She's doing very well," the doctor reported on the patient. "The antibiotics are working, and the fever is almost gone. Her vital signs are strong and definitely improving. I've given the okay for her to be moved into a private room in this wing, which is attached to the intensive care unit."

"That's great. So the liver is functioning again?" Jeff asked, sensing more than the doctor was saying.

Dr. Matherson looked grave. "That's the most serious issue at present."

Jeremy glanced at the other two. His uncle was staring at the doctor. Zia stared at her hands, clenched together in her lap.

"How bad is it?" Jeff asked, his face set in grim lines.

An expression of grief held in, controlled by an iron will, Jeremy acknowledged, feeling the tightness in his own facial muscles.

When the doctor hesitated, Jeremy knew the news wasn't good.

"She's stable," the IC resident said in the careful way of those who don't want to build false expectations. "We'll have to see how her body responds."

"And if the liver can regenerate itself," Zia concluded. "Is there enough left to do that?"

"The surgeon thinks there is."

"What if there isn't?" Jeff asked.

"We would need a donor with matching blood factors for a transplant. Ms. Aquilon would be a prime candidate for the procedure. Fifty-three isn't old and she's in very good health. With your permission, the hospital will add her name to the waiting list for a donor," he said to Jeff.

"Yes, of course," Jeff said at once.

"I'll have someone from administration bring the forms up. In the meantime, she'll remain under observation, but we're taking her off the ventilator. She's resting well and we'll let her wake naturally. You can stay with her," he advised.

When the doctor left the room, Zia also went out. She pulled the door closed behind her.

Jeremy wondered about the length of the list of those waiting for a donor organ.

Suddenly he heard Zia's voice. It sounded as if she were in a well, one located in the room. He realized the words came from the air vent in the ceiling over the door. She and the doctor must be standing near a similar vent in the hallway.

"If a living person matched, could that person give my mother part of her liver?" she asked.

Jeremy and his uncle exchanged a startled glance as they waited for the answer.

"Yes, that's entirely possible. It's been done a number of times," the doctor said.

"That's what I heard. What about the surgical team here?" she asked. "Could they do it?"

Dr. Matherson paused, then said, "I can check."

"I'm her daughter," Zia said. "We have the same blood type. I should be a match."

"It takes several factors to be a donor. We'll see," the doctor hedged. The gravity of his voice indicated his concern. "I would rather find an organ donor. Any time a person undergoes surgery, it can be dangerous."

Zia spoke impatiently. "I realize that, but she's my mother. I should be the one who—"

When she stopped abruptly, Jeremy stood and clenched his fists, experiencing a nearly overwhelming urge to go to her and share her distress.

"I want to do this for her," Zia finished. Her brief laugh was sad. "I owe her so much. Will you call the surgical team right away…in case we need to act quickly?"

Dr. Matherson spoke assuringly. "As soon as I get to the office in the morning. I'll report back to you as soon as I talk to the surgeon and Chief of Staff here at the hospital."

After the doctor left, Jeremy and his uncle shared another glance. Jeremy knew the same thought had occurred to both of them—maybe Zia wasn't the self-centered only child they'd first met fourteen years ago.

When Zia returned, the three went together and

checked on Caileen, who had been moved to the new room. As the doctor had said, the ventilator was gone and she seemed to be sleeping peacefully. A tube was clipped to her nose. Her heart rate and blood oxygen level were still being monitored.

Beside him, he felt a tremor run over Zia as her arm brushed his, and he gave her a quick glance.

"She looks better," Jeff said. He tried the chair that opened into a bed. "This will be comfortable for the night. You two should go to the inn. You need some rest, too."

After making sure Jeff had their cell phone numbers handy, Jeremy drove to the inn. He paused at Zia's door.

"Call if you wake up first," he told her. "We'll have breakfast here, then head back to the hospital early."

"Thank you," she said in a low tone, managing a smile of such open gratitude, it surprised him. "Thank you for coming with me and for helping with everything today."

"Hey," he said, feeling oddly gentle toward her, this woman he'd thought distant and not terribly caring, "we're a team. All for one and one for all, and all that blarney, you know."

She nodded, her beautiful eyes as solemn as an owl's.

"Families help each other," he said. He thought of her volunteering herself as a donor for Caileen. Unexplained tenderness washed over him. Damn, but he didn't understand his own feelings anymore, much less hers.

"Good night," she said and went inside.

After he entered his room, he felt restless, unable to relax. Next door, he heard her shower come on. Images sprang to mind—of them together, warm water running over their naked bodies while they touched each other and found relief from tension in the mind-numbing release of passion.

While he'd acknowledged her beauty long ago, he'd never dwelt on it. He'd had other irons in the fire, such as graduating and establishing his career, and hadn't spared much thought to the lovely but oh so distant goddess who appeared on rare occasions in their lives.

One thing he'd learned during this dangerous illness—Zia was a deeper person than he'd thought. Did that mean she was as lovely inside as she was on the outside?

Chapter Five

Zia woke at six when the alarm went off. With a groan, she forced her reluctant, stiff body from the comfortable bed, knocked on the wall and heard Jeremy call out that he was awake, then washed up and dressed for the day.

Ten minutes later, she heard his voice through the doors, each with its own lock, that joined their rooms.

"I'm ready," she announced, opening her door and finding him standing in the open doorway on his side.

The fresh scent of his aftershave wafted over her and she couldn't help noticing that Jeremy had matured into a wonderfully attractive package of masculine good looks and easy charm. Those, coupled with his caring nature, would make some fortunate woman very happy someday.

Where was the man who would make *her* very happy?

Swallowing hard as undefined emotions rushed over her, she forced herself to smile brightly. Maybe someday she would find that person. It wouldn't be a one-sided affair. She wanted to share her life and love with that special person, the one she could trust with all her heart…but where was he?

When she and Jeremy went into the breakfast room at the inn, she caught sight of them in the mirror behind the breakfast buffet. Her blond hair and fair skin formed a striking contrast to his darker hues. They were a notably handsome couple. Across the way, she saw the man behind the reception desk observing them, envy in his expression as he glanced at Jeremy, then back to her.

Men tended to fall for her looks without knowing her at all, she mused, aware of Jeremy's gaze on their reflection.

She'd learned over the years to hold herself aloof from such instant attractions. Some men, even though she was careful not to lead them on, became angry when she didn't respond to their overtures. They acted as if she owed them something for their attention, which was superficial at best and unwanted on her part.

She'd been called a "cold bitch" more than once in her life. Gazing at her and Jeremy's images, she suddenly wished for things to be simpler. If she looked more like her mother, who was pretty, rather than her father, who was handsome as sin….

Her dad had been married—and divorced—three

times. Did women expect more of him because of his Adonis looks?

"You're everything bright and sunny this morning," Jeremy said.

"And you're everything dark and dangerous," she answered with a smile, needing to put them on a lighter plane even as her breath became shallow and her pulse speeded up.

"Oh, right," he muttered wryly at her assessment, flashing his megawatt grin at her through the mirror.

She found herself still smiling as she prepared cereal, then gave in to the temptation of a chocolate-covered doughnut. Jeremy, she noticed, didn't hesitate over using the waffle iron that produced a perfectly cooked round in a couple of minutes.

"Wish I had one of those at home," she told him.

"Frozen ones are pretty good, too." He held the fork out to her and let her take the first bite of the treat.

"Really delicious," she told him.

They ate quickly, then decided to walk the block to the hospital rather than find another parking space.

On the third-floor wing next to the ICU, they found Jeff looking fresh and rested. Baskets of flowers and fruit lined the windowsill, turning the room into a garden.

Her mother was sleeping, but delicate color warmed her lips and cheeks and the oxygen tube was gone from her nose.

"Has she woken up yet?" Zia asked.

"Yes, we talked about an hour ago. I told her you two were in town," Jeff told them. "She said we weren't to worry, that she was fine. However, when the nurse asked if she needed a painkiller in the IV, she said yes. She's been asleep since then."

"She looks so much better," Zia murmured.

Jeff chuckled. "She made me brush her hair and give her a toothbrush and warm washcloth before she would take the pain medication. She said she didn't want to scare you kids by looking like a witch."

Zia laughed even as she felt the quick burn of tears behind her eyes. That was so like her mom, concerned about other people's feelings and impressions. She leaned over and planted a kiss on the cool forehead, glad that the fever seemed totally gone.

"Have you eaten?" Jeff asked.

"Yes, at the inn," Jeremy said.

"Good. I think I'll go to the cafeteria now that you're here. I didn't want to leave in case the doctor stopped by."

"Why don't you go with him?" Zia suggested to Jeremy. "I'll stay. It'll make me feel useful."

When he nodded and followed his uncle out of the room, Zia pulled a straight chair close and propped her feet on the side rail of the bed. She stared out the window at the bright sky and felt an unexpected lift to her spirits.

Jeff, Jeremy and the doctor arrived at the same time forty minutes later. This time the medical professional was the hospital Chief of Staff for surgery, an older woman who looked matronly and capable. Her name was Dr. Cohen.

"So you want to be the donor if we need one," she said, assessing Zia.

"If possible."

Jeremy spoke up. "I'll volunteer, too. My blood is O-negative, so I may be a candidate."

"Same here," Jeff said.

Dr. Cohen smiled at all of them. "The lab has checked her liver enzymes every four hours since surgery. The levels are good, not normal yet, but we think there's regeneration going on."

"You can tell already?" Jeff asked.

"I've known patients who regrew fifty percent of a damaged liver in a week. It's an amazing organ."

Zia spotted the sheen of moisture in Jeff's eyes before he turned away and brushed a hand over his face.

"It's strictly a waiting game now," the doctor continued. "By tomorrow, if there's no resurgence of the fever, we can consider her out of the woods."

"How long before she's well?" Jeff asked.

"Six to eight weeks of rest and she can resume her normal activities."

"Are you talking about me?" a cheerful voice interrupted the murmurs of relief from Jeff, Jeremy and Zia.

"Hey, girl," Jeff said, stepping up to the bedside and taking her hand. "You gave us a scare."

"I told you I was okay." Caileen looked past him. "So, besides a wedding, this is what it takes to get you two home?"

"Don't give her any more of that painkiller," Jeremy advised the doctor. "Another day, and she'll be impossible to handle."

Zia heard their laughter and her own as if it was far

away. An odd lightness made her feel she was floating. She felt for the chair she'd sat in earlier and slid onto it. She'd never fainted in her life and she wasn't starting now, but the relief at hearing her mother's voice was greater than she'd expected.

While Caileen slept off and on most of the day, the atmosphere in the hospital room was much brighter. Jeff and Jeremy discussed their work and the state of the world while Zia was content to mostly listen.

When her mother declared she was starving and was peeved when told she'd have to wait until the doctor gave approval for her to eat, Zia had to laugh. It was a relief to know Caileen was getting back to normal and wanting food.

Zia caught Jeremy's eyes on her. They grinned at each other like conspirators after a successful job. She felt like laughing for no reason but pure happiness.

Her mother wasn't totally clear of danger, but hope bounced around inside Zia with the verve of a Ping-Pong ball.

At nine that night, after Caileen had a cup of broth— they were still giving her liquids through the IV—Jeff told them to leave. He was ready for bed.

"I have two beds in my room at the inn," Jeremy told him. "We can share. Or I can stay here tonight while you get some rest."

His uncle shook his head. "I'll sleep better knowing what's going on."

A few minutes later, walking down the street in the dusk, Zia said softly, "I'm glad Mom found Jeff."

"They've made a good life together," Jeremy said.

"I resented her newfound happiness at first. I was jealous that her life was coming together while mine…" She tried to laugh, to show it didn't matter after all this time, but the sound came out sort of croaky. "…mine was falling apart."

"That's natural," he told her.

"You're so diplomatic."

At her door, she stopped and gazed up at him.

"What?" he asked, his manner wary, his expression one of perplexed amusement.

"You're a lot like your uncle," she concluded softly.

"He's a hundred times better than I'll ever be."

She shook her head, then on an impulse she couldn't control, she laid her hands on his shoulders and reached upward until she could touch his lips.

She felt the tension enter his body, then the lift of his chest against hers as he sucked in a harsh breath. His arms swept around her and she was encased in his embrace.

So warm, she thought. *So…welcoming.*

She arched upward, pressing closer, wanting more. The kiss escalated, becoming one of passion. She stopped thinking and, for a time out of time, let herself simply enjoy the human contact and all the sensations that went with it.

His woodsy scent seemed to form a cocoon around her, shielding her from a world that had never seemed kind. She leaned into him, experiencing his strength wherever they touched.

Muscles flexed and hardened. She wrapped her arms

tightly around him and felt the merging of their bodies—curves and planes meeting and melding, flesh conforming to flesh, all so naturally she didn't even have to think about it or figure out why or consider the thousand other questions that usually came to mind.

When his tongue stroked her lips, she opened to him and shared the moist intimacy of their mouths with an eagerness she hadn't known in years. His hands, large and gentle, caressed along her back, soothing yet exciting. He alternated the pressure of his palms against her skin, at times a brushstroke barely felt, then suddenly becoming harder, urging her closer, making her yearn for completion.

She knew that wasn't going to happen.

For a moment, sadness engulfed her, then she sighed and moved just a tiny bit, the slightest distance from him.

He at once stepped away. His frown was one of stunned anger, as if he couldn't believe what had just happened, and with *her*, of all people.

"Zia, my God, I'm sorry," he murmured. "I didn't mean to come on like that. I don't know what I was thinking—"

"It's okay," she said, not wanting to hear his shock, his apology. "It's because we're tired…and relieved," she added, needing to believe her own intentions were innocent.

"Yeah. We've both been under a lot of strain lately with new jobs and moving, then Caileen's illness. Anyone would go off the deep end in those circumstances."

"Right," she agreed, grabbing his explanation as if it

were a lifeline. She quickly unlocked her door, bade him good-night and went inside. Perversely, she wished he hadn't come up with so many excuses for their unwise behavior.

Young and foolish.

Would she ever be like that again? Would she ever feel that confident with another person?

Probably not.

But in his arms, for those few minutes, she'd felt so right…so wanted…cherished.

Jeremy heard the water flow through the pipes next door just as he stepped into the shower the next morning. His body reacted immediately. The ache in his groin became one in his gut. It was one thing to act like a lech in his dreams, all of which had been torrid last night, but to act that way with Zia….

He groaned at the memory even as his body grew harder and more eager for the completion that sizzling kiss had demanded.

Damn, he couldn't figure out how it had happened. She'd moved first—he was pretty sure she had—then, well, he'd done the rest.

He cursed again.

After spending an hour or two doing some intensive analysis when he was in bed, he'd decided Zia's impulsive kiss had been just that—an urge born out of relief and gratitude that her mom was doing so well.

He was the one who'd taken it too far.

Grimacing at the desperate hunger that had overtaken common sense, he stepped into the stream of water and soaped up. His libido, he admitted, didn't give a damn why she'd turned to him. It was just delighted that she had.

The night had been one long wish for fulfillment as his dreams rode the river of desire without end. He'd been more than aggravated that he couldn't turn them off and enjoy the sleep of an innocent.

Innocent. Ha. One taste of her mouth, and he'd been damned. The gentle yielding of her body against his had dissolved any caution on his part. For about ten seconds, he'd felt she was *his*. Worse, there was still some part of him that wanted to claim her, to tell the world to back off, that she was his woman.

It would be a thousand times harder to be around her and not remember…not want….

He flipped the faucet to cold water only.

Twenty minutes later, he answered the knock between their rooms and opened the door on his side.

"Ready?" she asked, looking as chirpy as a robin in red slacks and a white knit top with a red-and-white beaded necklace and earrings to match. Her sandals disclosed red toenails, the sight of which sent a shaft of hunger through him again.

Man, he was losing it.

"Yes. You want me to make you a waffle this morning?" he asked, needing something to focus on so he wouldn't dwell on her luscious red lips, the swell of her breasts under the top, the curve of her hips….

He groaned internally.

"Would you? I must admit I've been wanting to try one since you gave me a bite of yours yesterday."

On that chummy note, they went to the breakfast room. She poured coffee and juice while he baked waffles for each of them. At the table, they looked over the local paper and listened to the headlines on the national and international news on TV.

The latest fashions were also in the news. "Where would any sane person wear something like that?" Zia commented on a denim outfit that looked as if it would fall apart in a strong breeze.

"Well, maybe doing yard work," he suggested.

They chuckled and went back to reading. He refilled their cups, then looked over the sports section of the paper. Zia called her father and told him about Caileen's illness, then discussed her plans for the new job. After hanging up, she read the book reviews in the paper and the business news.

The scene reminded him of weekend mornings when Jeff and Caileen had lingered at the table after he, Tony and Krista went about their own pursuits. The couple had liked to read news stories to each other and comment on them. At the time, it had seemed "senior citizen" stuff to him and his cousins.

A surprising sense of loss came to him. He realized how much he missed those mornings, that sense of caring people around him and the other two, surrounding them with love. In pursuing his career, he'd set other things aside—companionship, commitment, love—so he could focus on making it in the world.

Another couple, near his and Zia's age, settled at a nearby table, interrupting his introspection and his enjoyment of lingering over coffee with a beautiful woman.

"I'd rather go to a museum," the other woman said peevishly.

"I want to hike some more." The man opened a map. "I thought we could ride up to the top of a ski run and explore the area, then have lunch at the lodge when we get back down."

He and Zia pretended not to hear the other two argue about how to spend the last days on their trip.

"Shall we go?" he asked as soon as Zia finished her waffle.

She nodded.

Walking the block to the hospital, he noticed the brightness of the morning, the chirp of birds in the trees. "The couple at the inn should come outside. On a day like this, all seems right with the world."

"Then you get to the hospital and realize it isn't that way for everyone."

He nodded. "When I was little, before my father died, I had a dog I loved. He was my age, but in dog years, he was old. My dad and I used to take him outside so the sun would ease his arthritis." He paused, remembering, then said softly, "Buster and my dad died the same year. It was like the end of an era."

"You lost two things you loved," she said.

He cleared his throat, self-conscious about disclosing so much about himself and wondering why he had. It wasn't his usual manner. "What I was getting at was the notion that we should bring all the patients out into the sun. It seems that would make them feel a lot better than being cooped up inside."

"I agree. Didn't hospitals used to have solariums for that reason? It seems I read about that in a book once."

"If so, it was a good idea."

When he smiled at her, she smiled back. The guilt, discomfort, whatever, over last night's kiss eased up. He held the door for her, then challenged her to a race at the bottom of the stairwell. She arched one eyebrow at him as if questioning his sanity, then darted forward.

They ran up the three flights of steps, arriving on the third floor breathless and exhilarated.

For a few seconds, walking down the hall to Caileen's room, he felt he could climb forever—as long as Zia was by his side.

Zia was delighted to find her mother sitting up in bed, looking as perky as the birds she'd seen on the way there.

Jeff was reading an article in the newspaper aloud, just as she and Jeremy had done that morning. The scene was so homey, she could have cried.

Naturally she didn't. Instead, she went to her mother and exchanged a hug. Then she did the same with Jeff, giving him a harder squeeze because she felt so grateful to him for being the person he was, for making her mom happy and for caring.

"Jeremy," Caileen said when the greetings were over, "take this man down and feed him or he'll be grouchier than a spring bear coming out of hibernation."

Jeff rolled his eyes. "Look who's talking. She's been demanding something more than broth since last night. The doctor said she could have soft food tonight if the enzymes continued to improve."

Caileen made a face. "Pureed baby food wasn't exactly what I had in mind."

That made the others laugh.

After the men left, Zia clasped her mother's free hand. "They've taken out one IV and removed the monitors. That's a good sign. Has the doctor been in?"

"Yes, shortly after six. I don't know when he sleeps or visits with his family. Speaking of family, Tony and Krista have both called. They said to tell you and Jeremy hello. Krista and Lance are leaving France this afternoon for Italy. They're visiting an appliance manufacturer there. Tony and Julianne shared the news that she's expecting. They're very excited."

"That's great," Zia said sincerely. She really was happy for the two couples. They'd found their true loves.

She sighed and felt envious. Get over it, she advised. "What did the doctor say when he came by?"

"Things are looking good." Caileen wrinkled her nose as she smiled. "I could have told him that. I haven't felt this good in weeks. Now I'm feeling guilty about you and Jeremy dropping everything and rushing up here."

Zia pulled the chair closer and sat down so she and Caileen could chat easily. "Well, I was free since my job doesn't start until the second week of August. Jeremy talks to his supervisors by phone a couple of times a day, so that's no problem." She paused and pretended to consider, then said, "I can't see any reason for guilt at all."

"You should be looking for an apartment and getting settled in. And checking out your new office."

"I've done that. It's about as big as a broom closet, and the secretary was installed when the corner stone was laid for the building."

"That old, huh?"

"Age isn't the problem," Zia continued. "It's change. The federal program will force several changes that might be hard to accept."

"Such as?"

"Accounting, for one. We have to account for each project and every penny spent. We're going to do it by computer, using a program that I've found very efficient. It can download info from the school's banking account and reconcile the checks, then assign the costs to the correct accounts. I've opened a checking account in town, and I know the bank has encryption capabilities. There shouldn't be any problems."

Caileen gave her a sympathetic perusal. "Except for those who don't want to learn something new. Is that why the secretary worries you?"

Zia nodded.

"You and Jeremy should go home. You might want to ask her for help in getting the new system up and running before August," her mom suggested in her tactful way.

"In other words, enlist the secretary's help and get her on my side before the time comes to use the new program."

"Exactly." Caileen paused. "Jeremy can probably help you find a place to live. He must have lots of contacts through the highway department."

"I didn't really think about asking him. The bridge site secretary referred me to her cousin who's in real estate. We've looked at several places. Some are too expensive, some are too far out from town, some are hardly more than shacks. I'm going to look at apartments next week. The residence hotel is lovely, but too expensive to stay there very long."

"Maybe you could rent a bedroom from Jeremy until you find something. His place isn't very far out, is it?"

"No, less than three miles. It's charming, that is, the living area and kitchen are. I haven't seen the rest of it."

She told Caileen about the furniture and colors and that Krista had given advice via cell phone. After a few minutes, Caileen yawned, so Zia fell silent. After her mother went to sleep, she gazed out the window while images of a tall, lithe body, barely glimpsed in a dim hallway, tumbled into her mind. She inhaled a shaky breath.

Last night she'd awakened from a dream so real, she'd still felt the impression of his lips against hers even as she realized she was in her room, alone.

That kiss, she thought in despair. Why, why, why had she allowed herself to reach for him?

No matter how many times she asked the question, no answers ever came to her. To let herself need someone was foolish. She wouldn't lean on Jeremy, or ask him for any favors.

While her mother apparently thought nothing of her moving into his house, Zia saw the danger that Caileen didn't.

Like a sleeping tiger, the hunger had been awakened between them. Her fault. She touched her lips, remembering the passion, the need for fulfillment.

Pressing her hand to her forehead, she groaned internally as she tried to keep the memory at bay. The trouble was, the damn thing wouldn't stay locked away. Like something wild and with a mind of its own, it waited to leap out at her every unguarded moment.

Forcing the thoughts aside, she reminded herself that she'd learned one thing from her mother. Discipline. She had only to assert firm control, to say *no* whenever an inappropriate image leaped into her mind—

"Hey," a soft voice said behind her, causing her to jump.

Zia turned from the window. "Shh, she's asleep."

Jeff stopped at the foot of the bed and gazed at his wife. "She's so much better. I think you two can go home and get on with your lives. She'll fret about wasting your time if you don't."

Zia nodded. "You're right. Jeremy has a lot of responsibility and problems at the bridge site." She glanced at him. "We have to check out of our rooms before noon. Perhaps we should do that and plan on leaving, say, after lunch?"

Jeremy nodded. "I can pack up and take care of the bill this morning while you visit with the folks."

"Good idea," Jeff chimed in.

Zia agreed. "Leave my room charge on my credit

card," she told Jeremy, then chatted quietly with Jeff about business and the happenings in Idaho while Jeremy carried out their plans.

Later, they brought sandwiches and drinks up to the room and chatted with Caileen while they ate. She got a tray with broth and a high nutrition milk shake. At her groan, they laughed.

"Hey, you want me to sneak in a pizza before we leave?" Jeremy asked her, his grin wicked.

"Yes!"

"No way," the nurse said, entering the room. "I'll have to confiscate it. Also any baked goods." She checked the patient's temperature and blood pressure "You're looking good," she said before she left. "Pizza next week for sure."

On this cheerful note, Zia and Jeremy said their farewells and headed for the interstate highway that would take them to Salt Lake City, then the state road that would take them home. The low pressure system caught up with them, and part of the trip was completed in a heavy rainfall with lots of thunder for drama.

They took turns driving and spoke very little on the way, arriving at his home a few minutes before midnight. He followed her back to town and walked her to the outside entrance of her room and set her suitcase inside the door when she opened it.

"Let me know how the house search goes," he told her. "I'll ask around, in case someone at work hears of something."

"I think I'll look at apartments. There're some new condos going up north of town."

"That's a golfing community. It'll be expensive."

She suppressed a sigh. "Well, something will turn up."

"Right." He raised a hand in a brief salute of goodbye and moved away. "I'll be out at the Desolation Canyon site for the foreseeable future. We're still having problems there. The boss wants me to stay on top of it personally."

"Good luck with it," she said and stepped inside the door. "Thanks for your help and for going with me on the trip. You were super."

He paused a couple of yards from her. "Caileen means a lot to me. She helped Tony and Krista get back with Uncle Jeff. She filled an empty place in his life that we kids couldn't, although I was several years older before I realized that."

His smile warmed her heart as Zia nodded. After he left and she was alone in the pleasant room, she thought of the special realm that existed for a man and woman who loved each other.

Would she ever find that private haven for the heart?

Another thought came to her. Why hadn't Jeremy?

Lots of women were attracted to him. She knew that. He tended to concentrate on work and other goals, though. Maybe when he got his house completed, then he would focus on finding the ideal woman to live there with him.

He would be good with children. Tony and Krista had always turned to him for advice. When they'd lived on their own that year, they had depended on him completely.

A pang went through her as she washed up and slipped on a nightshirt. She wasn't good at trusting people.

Maybe that was why some of them thought she was cool and haughty. She didn't mean to give that impression.

After turning off the light, she lay in the dark, her mind not quite ready to shut down.

Jeremy had made it clear that he had no more time for her. He'd done his duty, as he saw it, now he had other business. His problems with the construction would keep his nose to the grindstone, or maybe she should say, the bridge embankment.

A smile tugged at her lips. Going out to the construction site had been fun. Everyone had been friendly. Because she was with Jeremy?

She could make friends on her own. But first, she reminded herself sternly, she needed to focus her energies on finding a place to live, then…then who knew? Maybe she would find everything her heart desired.

Whatever that was.

Chapter Six

For the next several days, Zia scoured the ads in the local paper for an apartment. She looked at several that were in people's homes, but ruled them out.

A couple of places were upstairs so she had to use the family front door and enter their living space to get to the steps. One had a separate entrance, but she would have to use the family kitchen to prepare her meals. Another was over a garage that looked so rickety, she feared it would fall down when she moved her things in.

She was used to having more privacy than any of those homes offered. Right, for all those romantic trysts she was sure to have as soon as she met someone special.

The apartments in the golfing community wouldn't be ready for at least three more months and, as Jeremy had predicted, were rather more costly than her budget allowed.

As the days crept by, she grew somewhat despondent about finding the perfect place. She'd settle for one that was adequate.

One bright note—her mother was doing fine. She'd gone home after nine days in the hospital, but she couldn't go back to work for two months and then only in the office. Naturally Caileen was fretting about the children and families under her care, but the rest was doing her good, she admitted.

Zia called every night until she got her phone bill, then she started watching her minutes more closely. It was nice to share the news of her day and catch up on hometown happenings.

July was hotter than normal, with the thermometer hovering around one hundred degrees day after day. On the Fourth, the inn held a picnic on the lawn for their guests. Later, Zia went to the town park and watched a baseball play-off between business leaders and city employees, including the mayor and off-duty firemen and police officers. The proceeds from the tournament would go for park equipment and a new drip irrigation system.

To her surprise, Jeremy was one of the players for the city. When he came up to bat, his blue T-shirt was plastered to his back and he wore a sweatband around his head. He had powerful arms and shoulders, so she wasn't surprised when he got a hit and made it to second base while another teammate scored.

There was something earthy and primitive about him,

she reflected. Elemental. As if he belonged to the land and its harsh beauty. He was candid and honest....

She recalled he'd said he would be staying at the bridge site while they solved the problems there. And that he used work as an excuse not to see a woman again. Which was the same reason he'd given her when they'd arrived back in town, that he would be busy at the work site. Okay, she could take a hint.

She wondered if there was someone sitting at one of the crowded tables on the lawn who was waiting for him. Not that it was any of her concern. She was merely curious.

She ate half a ball of cotton candy and tossed the rest, then meandered back to the inn before evening. While she was aware of stares from some local Lotharios, no one approached or spoke to her. She wondered if she wore a sign that said Beware or something equally off-putting.

Sitting alone on the side porch, she listened to the muted laughter of other guests who wisely stayed inside the air-conditioned great room and joined in high tea. After preparing a plate of tiny sandwiches and scones, she returned to her solitude.

All the people inside were either couples or part of family groups. Other than one panhandler she'd passed on the street, who'd been alone like her—no, even he'd had a scruffy dog for companionship—everyone she'd seen that day had been with others.

No wonder some of her friends had married in desperation. The loneliness was hard to take, especially on holidays.

But she would be settled in an apartment soon, she

hoped, and in her new job next month, so all would be well. Being alone was something she'd learned to handle long ago.

Jeremy stood on the dusty track and observed the trail of the ambulance leaving the work site. The site secretary, who kept up with *everything,* was on her way to the hospital. He hoped she made it before the baby arrived.

It was going to be nip and tuck, as the paramedic had said, snapping on latex gloves and sitting beside the expectant mother, his manner somewhat hopeful that he would get to share in the excitement of the birth.

Images of long ago rose in Jeremy's mind. Zia, her deep blue eyes the only color in her face, pain drawing her pale lips into a grimace as a contraction racked her body. His own quickly suppressed fear that she would die….

Jeremy stuffed the memory into the black box of the past and returned to the office. Cool air flowed over him when he opened the door. Last week the air conditioner had quit, so he'd had to have it replaced ASAP. No one could work inside when the heat built up to a hundred and ten degrees or more.

Settling at Tina's desk, he tried to recall the instructions she'd given him as the medics had lifted her onto the gurney and taken her away. He found the checks that needed his signature, signed them, then frowned as he figured out which of the triplicate copies went with the payment, which went into the filing cabinet, and what the hell to do with the third.

After finishing what had to be done with the paperwork, he went to the engineering trailer and studied the core samples of soil he'd had pulled on each side of the gorge. The higher-ups hadn't liked it, but the pilings had to be drilled deeper and the pier foundations extended back from the edge another five feet.

Delays cost money. Fortunately, the federal funds had come through and plans to open up the national forest area to camping and hiking could go forth.

The rest of the day was spent in meetings with the site engineer and supervisor to make sure all of them were on the same track. They figured out the best work plan, then he headed for town and the mountain of paperwork that awaited him there.

Sheesh, he could get twice as much done if it weren't for the reports that went with the job.

Zia stared at the members of the school board as if they were speaking a language she didn't know. "No state funds?" she repeated, not understanding the situation at all.

"The state was supposed to match the federal funds," the head of the county school administration explained. "So we don't have the money for your salary."

"Not even for one year?" she questioned.

"We're very sorry," the chairman of the school board said. "We're as shocked as you are. We thought it was a done deal when the federal funds came through."

"What about my contract?"

"Well, since you haven't started yet, we'd hoped you would consider it, uh, null and void."

His expression indicated he expected her to agree without giving them any grief.

Zia stood and looked at each of the board members and the superintendent. "Gentlemen, I gave up a perfectly good position to come here. I moved out of my apartment and put my furniture in storage until I could find a local place to live. We signed an agreement. The breach of contract clause becomes effective if you renege. I want to make sure you understand that."

"We don't have the money to pay for work that isn't performed," the chairman said coldly.

"I'm here, ready and able to do my duties."

"We'll have to talk to our attorney," the man stated.

Zia smiled, not at all intimidated. She was used to dealing with bureaucrats on the federal, state and local levels in her work. "You do that. Be sure to point out the contract became effective upon signing last May, not upon starting the position.

"Since you'll have to pay an equivalent of six months wages to break the contract, why not use that money to pay my salary instead," she suggested. "Maybe you can convince the state to come through during that time, or else find the extra money somewhere else in the budget. This program is too good to be dropped." At the door, she added, "You have my cell phone number. Unless I hear otherwise or receive a check for full payment of the breach of contract, I'll be in the office the second week in August."

Leaving the building, which was new and modern—where had they gotten the funds for construction, just tell her that!—she continued up the street toward the inn.

The sun beat fiercely down on her face as she exhaled and tried to ease the stress caused by the interview. When the school board had asked her to come in for a meeting, she'd been prepared to speak on the curriculum changes and the computer accounting program she would install on her own time and teach others to use according to federal regulations.

Recalling her enthusiasm and the fact that contract clauses had been far from her mind, she sighed and felt her spirits slump all the way to the hot pavement under her beige flats.

Truthfully, she felt betrayed.

It wasn't the first time, she acknowledged as she arrived at the inn and went inside to change to shorts and a T-shirt.

After preparing a glass of iced tea, she went out on the porch in her bare feet and sat in a wicker rocker, lost in memories of other times, other places.

When she'd been four and had realized her father was leaving her and her mom, she'd sobbed and clung to his waist, refusing to let him go. He'd removed her clinging arms and set her away. He'd told her he had work in another state, but he'd be back.

He hadn't returned.

At nineteen, Sammy had made it clear he liked having her for his steady as long as there weren't any complications. He'd split as soon as there were, and her tears hadn't made a sliver of difference when he dropped her at her house and left without a backward glance.

She'd learned to never, ever display emotion when dealing with disappointment, disillusionment or the deepest hurt to the heart. Another sigh escaped her, a long, slow one that bordered on despair and regret and a thousand other useless emotions.

Get over it, she scoffed impatiently.

She could certainly live with the frustration of losing a job she hadn't even started. Now it was simply a question of finding another one so she could eat, afford a place to live and enjoy similar little luxuries, she thought facetiously.

"Maybe tomorrow," she murmured, then pressed the cool glass against her brow and sighed yet again. Tomorrow. She had to believe tomorrow would be better.

She'd arrived in town in the middle of June. It was now Monday, July 17. She'd paid another two weeks rental for her room on Saturday, sure that she'd find a place before the month was up. Where, she wondered, had such misplaced confidence come from?

She would have laughed, but she was suddenly afraid it might end in a sob. She wouldn't cry. She wouldn't.

On Wednesday, Jeremy cursed and threw a pen across the trailer. It hit the wall and disappeared behind a file cabinet.

He heaved a frustrated breath, pushed the chair back and headed for town. First lunch, then a budget meeting with the state accounting guru, which would take all afternoon.

In town, he found a parking place under the shade of a tree at the DOT building, his only piece of good luck since Tina went to the hospital a week ago and delivered a tiny boy that was over two months early. Both mom and child were doing well.

Too bad he couldn't say the same about himself. Slamming the truck door, he headed for the soup and salad restaurant. From the periphery of his vision, he caught sight of a familiar figure.

"Hey, Zia," he called.

His breath literally died in his throat as she turned toward him. Dressed in white shorts and a blue top, her hair in a ponytail that shifted in the usual afternoon breeze that came down from the mountains, she looked like every adolescent boy's dream-come-true.

Huh. He wasn't a kid, but his heart was hammering like a steam engine with one piston. It had taken a couple of weeks before he'd stopping dreaming of her after that kiss when her mom was in the hospital.

"Hi," she said, stopping a few feet away.

"Uh, I'm on my way to lunch. Care to join me?"

Her hesitation was so visible and so lengthy, he felt a spear of anger shoot through him. What was with her anyway?

"Well, you must have other plans," he said and started off. He wanted to eat before he faced hours of budget discussion.

"No, wait. I—I don't know why I, that is, yes, lunch would be nice."

He managed a smile and tamped down the temper. It seemed Zia was back to normal—distant and aloof. Okay, he could handle that.

Falling into step beside her, he pointed toward the small

restaurant. She nodded. Without words, they went inside, ordered and paid for their food before selecting a table.

Jeremy felt a little funny inside. He'd seen Zia check her wallet and lay out the exact change for her lunch. He hadn't offered to pay because in the past she'd refused with a haughty, closed look on her face.

"I suppose you've found a place to live?" he asked, adding three packs of sugar to his large iced tea.

"Actually, no," she replied, without looking at him. She squeezed a slice of lemon into her water glass. "I'm not sure I'm going to stay in the area."

He tried to figure out exactly what this meant, but gave it up. "You decided you don't like the town?"

She shook her head. Her smile was cool, remote. "The job isn't going to pan out."

"What happened to the three-year contract?"

If he hadn't been watching closely, he'd have missed the slow, deep breath, as if she sought control, before she spoke.

"The funds didn't come through, so I guess the position is out. The education board wants to cancel."

"Can they do that?"

"Not legally, not without paying the penalty." Her laughter was brief and sardonic. "The problem is that I keep remembering how strapped schools are for money and feeling guilty about it."

"What about you? Are you okay for money?"

She pressed her lips together, then smiled again. "It makes me nervous to live off savings. I remember how hard it was for Mom to pay the bills when I was young.

Once I woke up and heard her crying. The bills were spread out all over the table. I'd had an asthma attack and she'd had to take me to the emergency room."

When she stopped, Jeremy stayed silent, absorbing the info.

"It was my fault we were short of money," she continued after a moment. "She used the food budget to pay for extra medicine that the insurance wouldn't cover. Maybe that's why I outgrew the illness. I knew we couldn't afford it."

Again the brief laughter from her, and suddenly the horde of tiny darts swarmed around his heart because he thought he heard more than irony. He heard guilt and pain and regret.

"About the contract," he said. "You have to live, too. The school board should have made sure they had all their ducks in a row before they signed on the dotted line."

"Yeah, that's what I tell myself whenever I start to call and tell them I'll negate the agreement."

He hesitated while wondering if he'd lost his mind. "You remember Tina at the bridge site?"

She nodded.

"Well, she had her baby last week, over two months early. She wants to extend her maternity leave to six months. I need someone to take her place, if you're interested. Until you decide what you want to do, or the school board comes through," he added, totally disjointed in his thinking.

She stared at him in stunned surprise.

"It was just a thought," he said dismissively. "A temporary job. Naturally you want to find something on your level—"

"No, no," she interrupted. "That sounds perfect. It would give me a breather…if you really mean it. I mean, can you hire me, or does it have to go through some hiring board?"

He chuckled. "I can replace the secretary. In fact, my boss said the sooner, the better. Things are in a mess."

"I don't know anything about the DOT," she told him.

"Well, that's my job. Your duties would consist of answering the phone, keeping people off my back, filing reports, tracking the accounts…general office stuff."

For the oddest moment, he thought he saw tears in her eyes. Nah, not Zia, he decided when she smiled in that cool, controlled manner she had.

"All right then." She held out her hand. "It's a deal, if you're sure you need me."

"I'm sure." Jeremy shook on it while doubts crowded into his brain. However, this would solve both their problems. Yeah. This would work. He thought of one more thing, hesitated, then decided what the hell—in for a penny, in for a pound. "Do you want to stay at my place? I got the spare bedroom finished. Uh, I don't have any furniture yet. You can pick out whatever you need. If you'd like to stay there. For a while."

Her mouth dropped open for a second, then she gave him a radiant smile. "I can pay rent," she said. "I insist."

* * *

On Saturday, Zia made sure she upheld her share of the load as she and Jeremy laid her queen-size mattress on the bedstead.

Instead of buying furniture, she'd asked to take her bedroom set out of storage and use it. When Jeremy had realized she was paying storage costs, he'd insisted they move everything to his place. Her kitchen and bath supplies, plus the living room furniture, were in the storage shed in the back of the cottage.

"There," she said in satisfaction, "that looks nice, doesn't it?"

Her chenille chaise, along with a maple table and reading lamp, were placed in the corner of the room. Windows on each side wall let in lots of natural light.

The walls were painted a soft golden yellow with a faux tan finish, making the room look as if it had mellowed with age rather than being brand-new and completed only the week before. She was pleased that her summer bedspread, a floral with pink and golden-yellow flowers on a blue background went well in the room.

Some throw pillows in blue, tan and yellow—maybe in a plaid to contrast with the floral—would bring the color scheme together. She would check the stores in town for them.

Against the wall opposite the chaise, a tall chest of drawers held her foldable clothing. A picture of Caileen and Jeff on their wedding day adorned the top of it.

"This was once part of a porch," Jeremy told her,

waving a hand to indicate her room. "Since this is the south side, I converted the deck to a screened sunroom. Next year, or the next, I'll add windows for all-year use."

"How nice," she said sincerely, envisioning it.

Her bedroom was to the left of the hallway. On the other side, behind the kitchen, was a laundry room, then a bath, which they would have to share, then Jeremy's room.

The hall split the house into two sections and ended at a door to the screened sunroom. A patio table with four chairs provided outdoor comfort. A gas grill was stored in a corner.

She wondered if he had plans for when he married and had children. Another bath and bedroom would be welcome. Not that it was any of her business. She stored the extra bedding she'd unpacked in the closet along with her clothing.

"Well," she said, "I think moving day is over. I'll have to call my mother and let her know. She was worried when I didn't find a place right off. Now she knows I'm in good hands."

Tossing Jeremy a teasing glance, Zia laughed and spun around, delighted with the room and at working out her difficulties with the school board.

She was going to work part-time for Jeremy until Tina returned and part-time for the education department, training the existing staff on the new federal program while the county made an appeal to the state to chip in the money to fully implement the new ideas.

No one knew it, but she'd also checked on her old position in Provo. While they'd hired someone to take her place, the superintendent had been delighted to put her name in the hat for the following year if an opening came up. He was still hoping to get funds for the new curriculum program, and if that came through, she could head it up.

So all was well, she thought in satisfaction, coming to a halt in front of her new landlord.

"I take it you're pleased with the room," he said, his wonderful smile breaking over his face.

Suddenly self-conscious at her giddy reaction, she nodded. "I didn't like being...unsettled."

He surveyed the results of their work. "So now you're settled?"

"Yes. For the present. I'll still look for a place of my own," she quickly assured him so he wouldn't think he had to put up with her forever. "But having a job and a place to stay that I can afford takes a load off my mind."

"Are you okay with the work arrangement?"

"Perfectly. Mornings at the work site, then afternoons in town seems ideal. By the time Tina returns, the other job may become full-time."

He nodded and glanced at his watch. "How about a sandwich? Then I've got to go out to the bridge for a meeting. You can ride along if you want."

"Good idea. I can look over the office while you're busy and check Tina's filing system. Different people use various methods, I've found. I don't want to mess things up for her."

He gave her a curious look as if surprised that she

knew this much about office procedures, or maybe about people. She'd learned a lot from her mother over the years, she could have told him.

As they left the forested area around Jeremy's home, and traveled south to the Desolation Canyon area, she took in the desert landscape as if seeing it anew. She noted the blooms on the prickly pear cactus, yellow like the sage blossoms, and drew in a deep breath as a sense of peace filled her.

"You like the desert," he said.

"Yes. In spite of being born in Southern California," she added. "Mom moved back to Idaho, where she was born, when she realized I needed a different environment, so I'm used to sage and scrub cedars. It's a bit greener back there, isn't it?"

"Yeah. The farther north or higher in the mountains, the more rainfall."

"Right." Since she couldn't think of any other topics of interest, she shut up and enjoyed the ride.

At the work site, she said hello to the two men waiting for Jeremy. Steve, the engineer, was in his mid-thirties. Gordan, the supervisor of the work crew, was probably fifty. They went to the engineering trailer while she went into the office.

For the next three hours, she filed the foot-high stack of papers in the to-be-filed box, read over the stuff in the in-box, looked over a stack of bills and unopened letters and made notes of questions to ask Jeremy. She also watered Tina's plants, dusted and straightened up the place.

When Jeremy entered the office, he stopped and gave an appreciative whistle. "This is the neatest the office has been in a year. Don't tell Tina I said that," he added in a stage whisper.

His praise did things to Zia's spirits.

"Ready to head home?" he asked.

The oddest sensation zigzagged through her chest at the question, an electric tingle like lightning but much more pleasant. Home. It had never sounded so good, even if it was temporary. Nodding, she grabbed her purse and headed out the door.

He flicked out the light, then checked that the door locked behind them.

"So how's the problem with the alternating layers of rock and soft earth going?" she asked once they were in the truck and bouncing over the dirt road that led to the main highway.

"Fine."

"What?" she asked when he flashed her a thoughtful glance.

"I'm surprised that you remembered. Few women of my acquaintance, unless they work for the DOT, recall things like that."

"Well, I worked for my father for three years while I finished my undergraduate degree. He built houses, but we still had to dig foundations and move dirt and rocks around. Since I'm going to be working at the bridge site, I took the liberty of reading some of the reports before I filed them."

"Good thinking," he murmured, looking pleased.

A glow seemed to spring up someplace inside her. In spite of a warning to herself not to take things too seriously, she couldn't tamp it down.

She wanted things to work out in this new place.

Chapter Seven

"*F*ire in the hole."

Zia, observing through the office window, put her hands over her ears as the warning of a dynamite blast rang out from Gordan, the field supervisor, over the bullhorn.

Earth and rocks flew upward, leaving a dust cloud behind as the heavier particles fell back to the ground. The afternoon breeze quickly dissipated the cloud. Gordan and Steve, the site engineer, cautiously approached the chasm to check the blast area.

Steve gave a thumbs-up to the crew. Everyone cheered, including Zia. She had to laugh at herself for getting excited about something so simple as a hole.

Gordan motioned for the dozer operator—Marti, the

woman she'd talked to at lunch when she'd visited the site with Jeremy—to start clearing the debris.

Still smiling, she returned to work and finished the filing, then the accounting entries. The routine was straightforward and very like the office work she'd done for her father while finishing college. She enjoyed putting things in order, and the people at the site were friendly and accepting.

Or maybe she didn't feel she had anything to prove and so was more at ease with them.

Three stacks of papers awaited decisions from Jeremy. She glanced at the clock. He was late, but that was no surprise. He'd had a budget meeting that morning with the state auditor.

The door opened and Marti's face appeared. "Hey, ready for lunch?"

"Yes. I didn't realize it was so late." She made sure the trailer key was on the stretchy band around her wrist, then walked to the mess tent with the equipment operator. During the week she'd worked at the site, she and Marti had become friends.

They selected their food and carried their trays to a long table, joining the other woman who worked with their crew. Sadie was eighteen and working as a flag man—flag person—for the summer before going to college in the fall to be a nurse. Her dad drove one of the big dump trucks that hauled away the excess dirt.

"How's it going?" Zia asked the young woman.

Sadie grimaced. "I nearly caused Marti to back into

my dad's truck this morning. I thought he was going to have a coronary."

"Men always overreact, especially with family," Marti blithely assured her. "He'll get over it."

"I hope he doesn't say anything in front of my brothers at dinner tonight. They'll crack a bunch of stupid jokes about it while my mom worries that I'll get myself killed."

Zia smiled as Marti consoled the teenager and told her stories about other new flag men, who happened to be male, and how they'd messed up.

"No one ever got maimed or killed," Marti finished in triumph.

Sadie swallowed a bite of her hamburger. "There's always a first time," she said, but she grinned, her spirits restored.

After she left, Zia said, "You're good with people, Marti. You know what to say to soothe their troubled souls. My mom's like that. It must be an inborn talent."

"Nah. I just remember what it's like being the only female doing a job with a bunch of men around and knowing everyone is watching for the least mistake. So, how's your mom doing these days?"

"Great. She's gardening during her time off and says they may have a hard time getting her to go back to work. But she won't be able to stay away from her kids and families for very long." Zia paused, then asked, "How does a person become wise?"

Marti studied her for a second. "Is that a personal question or a general one?"

"Both?" Zia shrugged. "I'm thirty-three. Why doesn't my life seem to be going anywhere?"

"Where do you want it to go?"

"I haven't the foggiest idea."

Marti made sympathetic sounds. "You're down because your expectations weren't met when you moved here. It has nothing to do with being wise."

"Good, because I've been feeling pretty dumb lately."

"Mmm, maybe something more is bothering you," the older woman suggested with a tiny smile playing at the corners of her mouth.

"What?" Zia finished the grilled chicken and vegetables and took a sip of iced tea.

"Have you fallen in love?"

The swallow of tea caught in her throat. After recovering from the choking fit, Zia managed a laugh and a retort. "Not that I know of."

"When I fell for my husband, I was in denial for months," Marti told her. "As a new hire and a heavy equipment operator, I had to prove I could make it in a man's world. It took a while to realize the world belongs to everyone and that I could also be a woman in any part of it."

"Where's your husband now?"

"He died in a hang fire three years ago. He was an explosives handler."

Zia knew that a hang fire was an explosion that didn't go off as it should, then blew up in your face when you thought the fuse had malfunctioned. "I'm so sorry. Jeremy didn't mention that when he said he lured you down here on the promise of a better life for you and your kids. I assumed you were divorced."

"The move was a new start for us, a place with no memories of happier times. The kids like it here, so it's working out."

"It isn't lonely for you?"

Marti studied her for a long minute, then sighed. "I'll always miss my Jimmy. But tonight, I'm joining the gang for dancing at a place out west of town. Why don't you come?"

"Oh, no, I couldn't."

"Give me one good reason why not."

At that moment, Jeremy walked in the mess tent and glanced around. When he spotted her, he came over.

"Hey," he said, settling into the chair next to her. He pushed his cap up and swiped across his forehead with his sleeve.

"Hi," Zia said and felt heat creep up her neck at Marti's quick appraisal.

"I saw you got the journal entries done," he continued. "That's a relief. The state auditor is going to pay us a visit this afternoon."

"If you're going to talk finances, that's my cue to leave," Marti declared. "My kids balance the checkbook for me. Oh, we're going to Beaver's tonight. Bring Zia. She'll need something to help her relax after dealing with the auditor."

"Good idea," Jeremy said.

To Zia, he sounded glum. Okay, she didn't expect cartwheels of joy, but did he have to frown so?

"That's okay. I really should, uh…" She tried to think of something she needed to do.

"It's fun," Jeremy told her, obviously asserting himself to be cordial. "They have live music every Friday night. Most of the crew goes. We can leave early if you get tired."

Marti stood and picked up her tray. "He's right. If you like to dance, this is the place. There's about ten men to every woman." She gave Zia a grin and left them.

"You really don't have to worry about me," Zia said. "I don't have to be entertained."

Jeremy glanced at her in surprise. "If you don't want to go, it's up to you," he said coolly. "Are you finished? The auditor will be here around one."

She accompanied him to the office, aware of a coolness between them that hadn't existed that week. Well, not that she'd noticed. Jeremy had come in late nearly every night. He had miles of road construction under his direction and the bridge site wasn't the only one having trouble. After hours, he stayed in town and caught up on paperwork, which he thought was mostly a lot of bother and not productive.

Wednesday night, when she'd suggested he bring home his rough draft reports and let her clean them up in the evenings on her laptop, he'd stared at her as if startled by the idea, then shook his head.

"You're not getting paid enough to take on more work," he'd told her.

She hadn't made any more offers to help. She'd eaten salads and sandwiches alone in the sunroom most evenings. A couple of squirrels had discovered she had a soft spot and would toss them bits of lettuce or carrots if they came to the screen door.

Often she was in her room for the night by the time Jeremy came home.

Friday afternoon passed quickly as the auditor, a middle-aged man who was all grim business, had her find invoices and lay out files of financial information for his perusal. The man totally ignored Jeremy, who studied engineering prints and listened to the brief conversations between Zia and the auditor.

At five, after the man left, Jeremy let out an audible breath. "I hope he doesn't stay around long. He makes me feel guilty even when I don't know what he's talking about, like I probably did something wrong without knowing it, and the cops are going to haul me off to jail."

"I'll bake you a cake with a file in it," she promised, then laughed.

He chuckled at her little joke. "Yeah, so I can hack my way out of prison. Thanks."

"Actually, the accounts are in good order. Tina kept very careful records, and everything is up-to-date, so you can stop worrying about it." She retrieved her purse from the bottom desk drawer and glanced around to make sure everything was in order.

"I'll follow you home," he said, going to the door and holding it open. "We'll go to the tavern around seven."

She nodded. "That'll give me time to prepare dinner."

"You don't have to cook for me," he said.

"My mom would be horrified if I didn't." She

laughed and glanced back over her shoulder at him as they headed for the parking area.

He stopped by her car. "It doesn't matter what the folks think. You pay for your room. You aren't required to do more."

"I know, but I have to eat, too, and it's more fun to cook for someone besides myself."

When he studied her as if she was some kind of strange specimen he'd happened upon, she smiled, waggled her fingers in farewell and headed home.

Dinner and dancing, she mused sardonically. It sounded as if she was going to have a romantic night.

Yeah, in her wildest dreams.

Jeremy parked beside Zia's car under the carport. He entered through the side of the house, unlocking the door to the kitchen and then following her in.

"I thought I'd wash the dust off before dinner. You need the bathroom first?"

She shook her head, her mind obviously already on her self-appointed task. He had a wary feeling about sharing a meal with her here at the cabin after a hard day at work. It felt too homey.

Stretching wearily, he went to the bathroom and turned on the shower. Glancing at the countertop, he had to admit she was very careful not to encroach on his space. None of her toiletries were ever left around the sink, not even a toothbrush. She carried her stuff back to her room after each use.

He stripped out of his dusty work clothing and

stepped into the shower. On top of the sliver of soap he'd been using—he kept forgetting to put out a new bar—was a pink one that smelled of exotic spices. He recognized the scent as one he unconsciously associated with her. It had been too subtle to identify, but at times he'd caught the elusive aroma and been intrigued.

Lifting the bar, he inhaled deeply, liking the spicy yet fresh smell. Looking at the size of the sliver, he realized she'd left the soap, probably thinking he was out.

He started to rub it over his chest when he spotted a short, curly, dark blond hair nestled in the soap. Images at once leaped into his inner vision—her standing in the stream of warm water, running the scented bar over her arms, torso, thighs, the delicate curve of her abdomen....

His breath lodged in his throat as his blood flamed. He tried to order his libido to calm down, but his instincts had taken over, functioning on the most primitive level, one of pure unadulterated desire for the woman who shared his home.

A very beautiful woman, yes, but she was more than that, he'd realized during the month she'd lived in Vernal.

He stared at the tiny curl, his mind spinning off on tangents of its own with no direction from him. Thinking of how soft her hair had been the couple of times he'd touched it, he knew she'd be soft all over...wherever he stroked...if she were in there with him...if they made love....

Muttering several curses, which didn't alleviate the situation at all, he laid the soap back on the dish and picked up the sliver. He managed to work up a lather.

After shampooing his hair, he rinsed and, wrapping a towel around his hips, headed for his room after making sure the hallway was clear.

Forcing himself to think of work and its problems— anything to take his mind off his strange attraction—he managed to dress in the local version of Friday night date casual. Fresh jeans with sharp creases down the front, his dress boots and a white shirt, the sleeves rolled up on his arms.

A call from one of his site supervisors claimed his attention for the next thirty minutes. When he opened the door and stepped out of his bedroom, he came to an immediate halt. Something smelled mouthwatering, and he knew what it was.

He headed for the kitchen.

Zia had her back to him as she removed a meat loaf from the oven. It was covered in a rich tomato sauce, the way her mother fixed it.

"Man, that smells great," he said. "Anything I can do to speed things along?"

She gave him a smile over her shoulder. Her face was flushed from the heat and curling tendrils lay against her temples and neck. His insides went to sizzling again in an instant.

"Would you set the table?"

"Sure." If he could manage to stand upright without embarrassing himself. Fortunately the island was between them.

He placed colorful mats on the table, then set out two plates and two sets of flatware. "What are we drinking?"

"Iced tea. It's on the counter next to the fridge."

She was whipping potatoes with the portable mixer. He had to ease behind her to get to the pitcher of tea. A whiff of her particular and very enticing scent made his senses reel. Gritting his teeth, he poured tall glasses of iced tea and quickly set them on the table, then sat down in his usual place.

In a minute, she placed the meat loaf, hot rolls, potatoes and a bowl of green beans in the center and two plates of salad at each place. The salad consisted of raw beets and squash, plus cashews and halved grapes, on a bed of greens coated with a tangy homemade dressing.

"This is delicious," he said, taking a bite of meat loaf after she sat down and indicated they should begin.

"Thank you." She gave him a pleased smile. "It's my mom's recipe. As promised."

"Except you're at my place instead of me being at yours."

Her face lost all emotion, as if a curtain had come down. "I shouldn't be here long. I check the rental ads every day. I—I'll try not to bother you."

Catching the uncertainty in her eyes, he realized, with startling clarity, that the closed manner she often displayed *could* be one of self-doubt rather than the haughtiness he'd always thought. He felt a prick of contrition. Had he misjudged her all these years?

Worse, had he and his cousins made her feel unwanted, the outsider who occasionally barged into their lives?

"Tina says the baby is growing like a weed," he said, picking a safe topic to ease the awkward moment.

"Did you see her?"

"No. She called the town office to make sure she could get the extra time on her maternity leave. She was pleased that you had taken over. I told her you were being careful not to mess up her filing system."

The smile returned, reserved now, as her smiles often were, but still, a smile. For some reason, he felt relieved. "I'll do the dishes while you get dressed," he volunteered.

She glanced at her navy slacks and white blouse. "This won't do?"

He shook his head. "Those jeans you wore on the trip to Boise to see Caileen would be good. The gals usually wear T-shirts, only they, uh, fit."

She looked down at her plate as if embarrassed or shocked or something. He couldn't tell for sure.

So what else was new? She'd always been hard to read.

Zia was aware of Jeremy's quick glance when she returned to the living room. She wore the snug jeans, as he'd suggested, and a stretchy red knit top, dotted with sequins, under a white-and-silver-striped shirt. Her earrings were fire coral, a gift from her father while on a surfing vacation to Hawaii. She'd pulled her hair to one side and fastened it with a sparkly clip.

Jeremy didn't say what he thought of the outfit. His silence made her nervous, which in turn caused her to clam up. On the trip, she hoped Marti was at the tavern before them.

When they arrived and went inside, the sudden dark and the deafening music caused her to stop. Jeremy nearly walked into her. His broad hands settled on her shoulders as he caught himself. Tingles ran down her arms, and she quickly stepped away.

"Hey, you're here," a familiar voice called out. "Come on, I've saved you a place with us."

Zia headed for Marti's table as her eyes adjusted to the dimness inside the popular bar. The place seemed packed with noisy, fun-seeking people. Some were couples but most were single guys, she noted.

It seemed every eye followed their progress across the room. Zia usually ignored stares, but for some reason she felt self-conscious and out of place tonight. She hadn't been so nervy since her first date. And this wasn't even a date.

Marti gave her, then Jeremy, a welcoming hug. "Grab a glass and help yourselves to beer."

Gordan, the field supervisor, stood, giving Zia an air kiss near her cheek and shaking hands with Jeremy.

Another couple left the dance floor and joined them. Zia recognized Cam, a young guy who also operated heavy equipment. He introduced his girlfriend, Shauna, who was flushed and giggly.

Both Shauna and Marti wore jeans. Shauna wore a short open knit sweater over a black fitted top. Her belly button was pierced. Zia felt better, knowing she was similarly dressed.

After settling at the round table, Jeremy poured them each a beer and refilled the others' glasses. They had to talk loudly to be heard over the band. When the fast number ended, Marti and Gordan went to the dance floor for a slow, moony tune of lost love and broken hearts. Cam and Shauna went, too.

Zia observed the crowded dance floor, picking out those faces she recognized from work. At the bar, the stag guys also looked over the dancers and seemed envious of the men with dates. Zia had already learned there weren't enough women for the bachelors in the area.

With logging, rafting and outdoor pursuits enticing men who liked outside jobs and-or recreation, there weren't equivalent lures for a lot of single females.

She smiled and nodded to two of the men she recognized. An hour passed. She nursed a glass of beer and wished she'd stayed at the cabin. She definitely didn't belong. No one had asked her to dance, although a couple of guys did come over and talk to them.

After they drifted off, she and Jeremy were alone at the table while the other couples danced. Neither spoke.

When it was time for refills on the pitchers of beer, Jeremy paid. Marti ordered two platters of appetizers. When the snacks arrived, Zia excused herself and went to the restroom.

Alone, she ran water over her wrists, then simply stood there in front of the mirror. She tried to smile, but her lips trembled.

This was like the first school dance she'd ever attended. None of the boys had approached her then, either, although she'd seen them laughing as they dared each other to ask her to dance. What, she wondered, was so wrong with her?

Okay, she could get through the evening, she told

herself, trying to bolster her sagging spirits. All she had to do was endure. She headed back to the table.

Only Marti and Jeremy were there. Coming from behind them, Zia realized they didn't know she'd returned when Marti spoke over the noise of the band. "You have to ask Zia to dance."

Jeremy didn't answer. Zia couldn't see his face to judge his reaction to this stern order. Embarrassment flooded her.

"The other guys won't ask her to dance until you do," Marti continued. "They don't know what the deal is with you two."

"There isn't anything between me and Zia," he stated.

"I know, but you need to break the ice, then I'll tell Gordan to dance with her. That'll make it clear to others that she's approachable."

Jeremy gave a sort of grunt. Zia didn't know if he agreed with Marti or not. She did know she felt miserable. She retraced her steps and came to the table from the side so they could see her and know she was in the vicinity.

Jeremy stood. "How about a dance?"

Pride almost made her refuse, curtly and coldly, but she nodded pleasantly, careful not to look at him or Marti. She didn't want them to detect any emotion in her eyes or the hurt, which was ridiculous, that she couldn't hide from herself.

On the crowded floor, she soon regretted that she hadn't taken off her overshirt. The vigorous two-step soon had her overheated. Jeremy was good at it, and when he saw she knew the steps, he led her into intricate turns.

After a bit, she lost her inhibitions and let herself enjoy the rhythm of the music. She loved to dance. When the tune ended, she headed for the table, aware of Jeremy behind her, his hand in the small of her back, which surprised her.

The band started a fast number. Gordan stood and glanced at Marti. She shook her head. "I'm going to have some fried cheese sticks while they're hot. Ask Zia."

When Gordan held out his hand to her, Zia took it and dipped into a curtsy. Okay, it was a setup, but she decided she didn't care. She would dance with anyone who asked and have fun if it killed her.

"Oh, wait," she said and removed the overshirt.

Turning to the floor, she saw the stag line at the bar look her over with renewed interest. She flashed a radiant smile as Gordan guided her into a twirl.

Her red sequined top didn't quite cover her middle. She saw Gordan glance at the coral studs she wore in her ears and the one in the edge of her navel. He gave her a conspiratorial grin.

She grinned back. She liked him and Marti. They weren't envious or threatened by her looks. They accepted her as they would any other friend. That meant a lot to her.

When the dance was over, she didn't make it to the table. One of the best-looking guys at the bar asked her to dance. She looked him over in a teasing but good-humored manner and nodded.

For the next four hours, she sat out a dance only if she insisted she needed to rest. Gordan and Cam each danced with her a couple of times. Jeremy sat as if made of stone.

She wanted to kick him, but she refrained. She *was* tempted to flirt outrageously with the stag crowd…or maybe with the great stone-face himself. She laughed at the idea while Jeremy eyed her suspiciously.

Jeremy washed down a cheesy potato skin with the last of his beer. He couldn't remember how many glasses he'd had. However, he didn't feel a buzz, so he thought he was okay.

He caught Marti's eyes on him. She covered her mouth and laughed about something. He gave her a smile, although he couldn't detect anything that was funny. He refilled his glass, then topped off Zia's.

"Oh, that was fun," she said, returning to the table after dancing with about a hundred guys.

He'd never noticed so many single men at the tavern before. They seemed to be coming out of the woodwork. Or maybe word had spread that the most beautiful woman in the whole damn state was there. And "approachable," to use Marti's term.

Not that he cared. Hell, no. It was nothing to him. It wasn't as if they were on a date or anything like that. Maybe he should explain to the other guys that, while Zia happened to be living in his house…and driving him crazy…she was free to do as she wished.

Nah, he couldn't do that. It wasn't couth, as Uncle Jeff would say.

He glanced at her while she took a sip of beer, wrinkled her nose, then chose the glass of ice water. Her face was flushed and glowed in the candlelight that flickered softly on each table. The red top showed off her curves to perfection.

And then there were the red earrings.

When he'd spotted the one in her navel, his blood pressure had shot into the danger zone. Luckily, he'd been sitting because he couldn't have stood up straight at that moment.

He'd wanted to leap to his feet and get her out of there before the dudes at the bar noticed.

But it had been too late.

They'd practically taken a number and lined up so they could claim a dance with her.

Not only that, but from being practically comatose for an hour, she suddenly sparkled all over the damn place.

His grievances with the evening piled up as she danced several times, her skill and looks leading to lots of envious glances in his direction. And more than one puzzled look as he sat stolidly in the chair and didn't dance again.

He frowned fiercely as a headache impinged on his heated thoughts.

"Are you ready to go home?" a soft feminine voice asked close to his ear.

He turned his head and gazed into eyes so perfect they looked like those big glass ones used in dolls. Her lips, rosy from laughing and talking, were so close he needed only move a fraction to claim them.

Not that he would. Nope. No way. He was a better man than that. He didn't give in to temptation. No, sir.

Just as he bent forward, she moved away and spoke to Marti. "I think we'd better go. It's after midnight. Jeremy probably has to work tomorrow."

"Nah," Gordan told her. "We got the weekend off now that we're down to solid rock for the bridge piers."

"That's not the only road in the state," Jeremy informed the other man. "On Monday, we have to move half the crew over toward Dinosaur National Park for road repairs. There'll be a rock slide during the next heavy rain near that double-S curve unless we shore up the slope."

Zia stood and slipped on the overshirt, hiding the two inches of smooth skin above her jeans. "I'm ready."

He sighed, tossed down some bills on the pile of change for the waitress, told the others good-night and headed for the door.

The single men shot him envious glances.

Yeah, well, things weren't going to happen the way they were imagining, he could have told them. Zia didn't let anyone that close....

Another memory flooded his mind. That night in Boise, outside her door, when she'd returned his kiss with a passion that had surprised the hell out of him, when she'd felt like warm honey melting in his arms, her lips the sweetest temptation he'd ever known.

At the SUV, she held out her hand. "Would you mind if I drove? I haven't handled one of these since I worked for my father."

The request took him aback, but he dropped the keys in her hand and held the driver's door for her. Once they were on the road, he studied her profile in the faint light of the moon.

"You seemed to have fun tonight," he said.

"I did. I haven't danced in ages. I'd forgotten how much I liked it. You're a good dancer," she added, flashing him her knockout smile. "I was surprised you didn't do more of it. Or is it that you don't like to dance?"

He shrugged, unwilling to offer an explanation.

The problem was he'd liked it too much. Her in his arms, moving to the same rhythm, their steps perfectly matched, as if they'd been dancing together forever....

The hunger pulsed through him, tormenting him with images, with ideas, with needs that were stronger than his sense of self-preservation.

Chapter Eight

The cottage was pleasantly warm, Zia noted, when they arrived home and went inside. The night air had cooled down to fifty degrees, and her overshirt wasn't quite enough to ward off the chill.

Or maybe it came from *him*.

She gave Jeremy a frowning glance and found him staring at her. "Does the crew go to Beaver's every Friday?" she asked in a friendly manner, handing him the truck keys.

"Some do, I suppose. The single guys trying to fill the time or score." He pinned her with a searing glance as he added the last word.

She stiffened. Was he accusing her of being flirty…or promiscuous? *Her*, the queen of the cold shoulder? As if.

However, she was determined to be so sweet, while living in his house, that bees would swarm to her.

"Do you go often?" she asked with just the right amount of interest in his life, not too inquisitive, not too cool.

She warmed a glass of milk in the microwave and took a couple of ibuprofen. Her legs ached from dancing so much. She leaned against the island counter, not at all sleepy, and not very happy, either.

So what else was new? When had happiness played a large part in anyone's life? As some wise person had said: It was a thing oft remembered but rarely experienced.

And, she mused, often looked back on from a time of duress, as youth was from the viewpoint of adulthood.

She'd been happy at the idea of a new start when she'd moved here, or so she'd thought, and now look where she was—jobless and homeless for all practical purposes.

Jeremy yawned and stretched. "It depends."

She finished the milk, rinsed the glass and stored it in the dishwasher. She knew, she really did, that she should drop the subject, but she asked in dulcet tones, "On what? Whether you're with someone you like?"

He sat down, tugged at his boots and tossed them to the side of the sofa. His glare would have melted an ice sculpture in ten seconds. "What the hell does that mean?"

She returned his gaze in kind. "It means you didn't want to go out tonight. It means Marti told you to dance with me. It means you sat there like a big grouch all evening."

He paced to the window and stared into the night. "So? You had a good time. Four hours of it."

"Plus an hour of being miserable and not knowing

what to do but sit there, smiling as if everything was wonderful."

"You're the one who seemed interested in going," he informed her, facing her with a fierce frown. "The tavern sometimes attracts a rough crowd. I didn't want any trouble."

"Neither did I."

"Yeah, but with your looks, if you'd gone alone, there would probably have been a fight over who got to put the make on you. When you arrived with me, that made things clear to everyone."

Her temperature went to a slow boil. "In the future, don't do me any favors. When I want a night out, I'm perfectly capable of going by myself."

"Fine. Then I can get some rest and not have to stay up half the night worrying about you."

She stalked over to him, looked him straight in the eye and said in a scathing tone, "I can take care of myself. Maybe I was a slow learner once, but I have fourteen years on my own behind me. I've learned a few things about men in that time."

He didn't answer. Instead his eyes fastened on her face, on her lips. She saw his chest lift, then he expelled the deep breath through gritted teeth. It occurred to her that he might be on the brink of losing control.

And, with a glance at the TV clock, that twelve forty-five in the morning wasn't a good time to have a confrontation...especially after four hours of being scintillating and radiant to show him she didn't care if he sat at the table in a snit.

"Dammit," he muttered.

Then...then she wasn't sure who moved first. In an instant, she was enclosed in his strong, demanding embrace.

His lips touched hers, pulled back as if burned, then settled into a blazing kiss.

She returned it furiously, biting at his lips, then stroking with her tongue. He groaned and pulled her closer, snugging them up against each other until no open spaces remained.

The urgency in his body flowed into her, becoming a sweet aphrodisiac, a thrumming in the deepest part of her. She wrapped her arms around his shoulders, molded herself to his strong planes and immersed herself in sensation. In delight. In something that almost seemed like happiness.

Jeremy forgot his grievances at watching, hour after hour, as Zia danced with one man, then another. There was only *now* and the fact that she was in his arms and it was everything he'd been dreaming about since that night at the inn in Boise.

Sliding his hands under the lapels of the shirt, he pushed it off her shoulders, down her arms, then tossed it toward the sofa. The formfitting top, with its shiny spangles, had enticed him all evening. He'd wanted to run his hands over it and explore her curves like a sculptor caressing a statue, one that embodied all that was feminine and lovely, the perfect image drawn from his imagination and the yearning of his heart.

Only Zia wasn't a statue. She was warm and real.

Very, very real. He traced the line of her torso with his palms and paused at the flare of her hips with two inches of bare, smooth flesh burning into his hands, branding him with the feel of her.

Moving back just a little bit, he examined the smooth coral stud in her navel.

"Jeremy?" she whispered.

There was the slightest question in her voice, as if she wondered what they were doing and if it was wise.

"It's okay," he said, gazing into eyes that reminded him of a mountain lake on a summer day, so blue, so inviting.

She nodded.

To his surprise, she closed her eyes and nestled into his arms again. Something welled up inside him, like a spring of hope or joy or something equally puzzling.

No. This was passion, pure and simple. It had been there between them for a long time, he realized. The tension he'd felt at the wedding, the way she'd gazed into space when they'd danced, the fact that each of them avoided the other when possible, those had been defensive mechanisms on their parts.

Zia couldn't remember experiencing such perfect bliss in her life. It had been waiting for her, all this time, and she hadn't known it, hadn't even thought it possible.

Don't do anything stupid.

Some cautious part of her mind repeated this mantra over and over, but she didn't want to listen. The wariness she always experienced in intimate situations was supplanted by a trust she hadn't felt in a long time.

The voice of caution faded into silence. She knew this man. She knew his integrity. It was as simple as that.

When his hands slid under her top, she shivered slightly as delight spread through her.

"Jeremy," she said, and this time there was no hesitation in her tone, only invitation.

"Let's get this off," he said.

"You, too," she demanded.

His smile did things to her.

With quick, impatient hands, they helped each other strip their upper clothing away. He bent to her breasts and paid equal attention to each with his lips and tongue.

She cupped his head and ran her fingers through his hair, liking the thickness, the sheen of the strands as they flowed between each finger. Against her hardened nipples, she felt the brush of his chest hair as he caressed her with a side-to-side movement of his body. Against her abdomen, his arousal incited her hunger to a higher pitch.

When he bent to her again, this time to tease her belly button and run his tongue around its edge, adroitly circling the stud she wore there, she discovered this was also an erotic place on her body. Electric tingles coursed through her with every caress from his mouth and his hands, which cupped her hips.

After an eternity in which her knees grew weak, he straightened and lifted his hands to her hair, then removed the clip at the side and slid his fingers into the waves.

With playful circles, her massaged her scalp, the back of her neck. "Relax," he murmured, a wisp of a smile floating over his mouth before he bent his head to hers again.

"I can't," she said against his lips. "I want you too much."

His chest lifted in a sigh. "That's what tonight was all about, wasn't it?"

"What?" She pressed her face against the side of his neck and tasted the slight saltiness of his skin with the tip of her tongue. She sucked gently, careful not to leave a red mark.

"The anger at the tavern. The argument when we got home. It was about this." He glided his hands through her hair, down her shoulders, then cupped her breasts. "I was jealous of the other guys dancing with you. I didn't want to admit it."

At his words, spoken in sardonic amusement, as if he laughed at their fate, the wariness returned. Male possessiveness. She'd run into that in the past. She eased back, then placed her hands over his, stopping the delicious stroking of her breasts.

"That's ridiculous," she said sternly.

"How else do you explain it?"

She thought of the men at the tavern, of Marti's smiling satisfaction when they crowded in, wanting to dance. Her spirits retreated to that distant place that was inside her, yet far, far away from her heart.

Men fell for her looks, not her. And she'd encouraged it.

Because?

Because she'd wanted Jeremy to notice her.

The truth was like a slap to the face. She'd used her physical appearance to entice him. Why else wear siren red to the dance if not to be noticed?

Physical attraction was shallow at best. Naturally it led to passion. And passion seemed to call out the worst in some men, as if she were a bone to be fought over. It certainly wasn't the way to that elusive state called happiness.

When she stepped back, he did, too. With a reasonable space between them, the hunger receded and common sense reasserted itself.

"You're right," she admitted in a low tone. "I was angry tonight. I'm not sure what triggered it. Maybe because you were so distant, and I resented it."

He surprised her by laughing.

"What?" she questioned, frowning at him.

"Welcome to the club," he told her. "I've often been irritated as hell because you maintained a space around you, as if you'd drawn a line and dared anyone to cross it. That's the way you were at the wedding, except maybe to Krista."

She nodded. "I didn't want anyone to come too close. You, Tony and Krista are family. When my mother married your uncle, she became an Aquilon. I was an adjunct to her, something extra that you couldn't exclude, but I...I didn't belong."

A stubborn expression came over his face. "You could have. If you'd wanted to. We would have welcomed you in."

"I couldn't." She sighed, picked up her shirt and

headed for her bedroom. "Except with Krista. Who could resist her? She was so sweet and loving."

"The rest of us weren't?" he asked, rather harshly.

"You were careful around me, the way you would be around someone known to go off the deep end for no reason." She managed a smile. "I was careful, too. I didn't want to trust anyone too much."

"But you called me when you needed help."

She paused in the hallway and nodded.

His eyes narrowed to slits as he studied her. "You trusted me enough for that."

"And been ashamed of it ever since. I got myself into a mess. I should have gotten myself out."

He seemed to think this over for an overly long time. The harshness left his face. "Hey," he scolded gently, "what are friends for?"

She had no answer. She'd never considered him a friend. Their lives seemed too entangled for something so simple as friendship.

"Good night," she murmured and headed down the hall.

Later, in bed, she stared toward the dark ceiling, lost in introspection as the strained relationship between her and Jeremy replayed itself over and over. She didn't know what she thought, how she felt. There was only turmoil inside.

But for a few seconds just before she went to sleep, she let herself remember what it had once felt like...to be young and foolish...and desperately in love.

* * *

Jeremy didn't usually have "morning after" regrets. He tried to play fair with people, but he was pretty sure he owed Zia an apology for the previous night. He'd been the worst kind of heel at the tavern. He smiled grimly. Nothing like having to tell a woman she was right in calling you a big grouch.

Her door was open, he noticed, as he headed for the kitchen. The coffee was made, but she wasn't there. He glanced around the living room just to make sure he hadn't missed her.

The empty feel of the house bore down on him. He shrugged it off. She was free to come and go as she pleased. He wasn't her keeper. But he sneaked a look out the window as he got eggs and bread out of the refrigerator. Her car was under the carport next to his SUV.

By the time he sat down to his breakfast, he was definitely annoyed. She could have left a note on the fridge—

At that moment, he heard the sunroom door open and close at the back of the house. A stir of cool desert air swirled through the house.

"Good morning," he called, relief spearing through him.

She came into the living area and smiled at him. "It is a good morning. I had no idea how lovely the view was along the ridge trail behind the house."

"You go for a run?" he asked, eyeing the sheen of perspiration on her face and the flush in her cheeks.

Nodding, she poured a cup of coffee, sipped, then

prepared a bowl of cereal and sliced a banana into it. She sat on the stool next to him at the island counter.

The exotic aroma of her soap and shampoo came to him, along with the fresh, outdoorsy smell of early morning in the high desert. He inhaled deeply, knowing he could pick her out of a lineup with his eyes closed. Her scent was embedded in his brain.

He took a bite of toast while hunger of a different sort pinged through him.

"What are you going to do today?" she asked.

"Whack the sage that's creeping too close to the house. I try to maintain a hundred-foot firebreak all around."

"Good idea."

She ate in quick, small bites, he noted. He recalled the taste, the feel, of her lips, a memory that had invaded his every dream during the night. He sighed.

"I think I owe you an apology," he murmured.

"For what?"

The question was unexpected. "Well, uh, for last night."

"For acting like an ass at the dance or for the kiss when we got home?" She cast him one of those cool, assessing glances she was so good at.

"Both, I guess," he said, sounding decidedly grumpy. "I thought women were supposed to know things like that. Aren't you supposed to have intuition about these things?"

"I don't take anything for granted." She finished her food and placed the bowl in the dishwasher, then disappeared.

The shower come on. Heaving a breath in exasperation, he polished off his eggs and toast, both of which were room temperature by now.

He knew he'd been wrong to act as he had last night, but should he have kept his mouth shut this morning?

It was one of those unexplained mysteries of life. Or of dealing with a woman he'd never understood. Same thing.

While Jeremy worked outside the rest of the morning, Zia devoted herself to the inside. In less than two hours, she had the furniture and floors shiny, the kitchen and bathroom sparkling.

Getting thoroughly into the domestic mood, she made an apple pie with a crunchy topping, then wondered what else she should do.

After changing her bed, she took the sheets to the laundry room. She stood there, lost in thought, while the washer filled.

Finally, she went to the back patio and called out to her housemate. After he turned the Weedwacker off, she told him she was washing sheets and asked if he wanted his included.

He gave her an unreadable stare from those midnight-dark eyes, then nodded.

While he returned to cutting down sagebrush, she went into his bedroom, then stopped as her heart suddenly pounded. She felt she'd stepped into a forbidden lair, one where she should tread softly and keep a sharp eye out for danger.

Which was ridiculous.

It was a perfectly innocuous room. The walls were sage-green on the top part. A glossy white beadboard wainscoting was on the bottom. A chair rail added an interesting architectural line.

The bed was king-size.

As it needed to be to accommodate his height, she reminded herself briskly. She stripped off the green-and-tan comforter and a tan thermal blanket. Two pillows with shams that matched the comforter were on the window seat, she noted.

Krista had probably picked out the set, and Jeremy most likely never put the decorative pillows on the bed.

Zia smiled as she recalled visits to the Aquilon household in which everyone helped get the house and yard work done. She'd been given chores, too, like the other kids.

Sometimes, on those visits, she'd felt she belonged.

She smiled in nostalgia for a time that had seemed simpler in some ways. Setting the past aside, she removed the linens, found clean ones and tucked them around the mattress. With the thermal blanket in place and the comforter over it, she placed the pillows with the matching shams on the bed, spotted two throw pillows in green, tan and white stripes, which matched the drapes, and placed them in front of the shams.

Standing at the door, she admired the effect, pleased with her work.

She bundled the used sheets in her arms. Carrying them to the laundry, she was immediately aware of the scent of his aftershave lotion. Also the soap he used, which had a piney smell. Underneath those was another aroma, one that was sort of musky and masculine and…and…

Closing her eyes, she inhaled deeply, lost in erotic memories of their shared embraces.

Maybe moving into his home hadn't been a good idea. Living in the same house made him much more *real*. Seeing him only on special occasions, well spaced from each other, she could forget he existed for months at a time.

A shaky sigh escaped her.

Once she'd wanted so much from life. She'd expected all her dreams to be fulfilled, as if it was owed to her. Being here in the cottage reminded her of those expectations. Her own existence, which she'd thought was fine before uprooting and moving here, now seemed lonely and pointless.

Hearing the kitchen door open, she quickly stuffed the bedding into the washer and closed the lid.

"Hey," he called.

"In here."

He came to the door. "I need to head into the mountains to check a couple of repairs. You want to come along for the ride? The scenery is great, and there's a barbecue place where we can stop for lunch."

"That would be nice. Are you leaving now?"

"I need to shower first. I got into some poison oak at the edge of the woods. I didn't realize it had sprouted there."

"Take your time," she told him. "There's a pie in the oven that needs to bake before I leave."

His smile was like sunshine after days of clouds, she thought, listening to his steps down the hall, then the sound of the shower. She remembered she'd left her soap in there.

When she'd left it earlier that week, because she'd thought the sliver in there too small to work up a lather, he hadn't used it. He probably didn't like the essential oils which gave it a delicious—in her opinion—scent of cinnamon, lavender and geranium with just a hint of cloves.

After reading an article in a newsmagazine, she heard the timer ding in the kitchen. Setting the apple pie to cool on the stovetop, she stood at the window and observed the wispy clouds collect over the mountains east of them.

"Man, that smells delicious," Jeremy said.

Her breath struggled in her throat as she turned and glanced his way. He was dressed in his usual jeans and a work shirt of blue chambray. He wore black athletic shoes and a white summer cowboy hat.

"Maybe we should have lunch here," he suggested, sniffing the air in an appreciative manner.

She shook her head. "That's dessert for dinner."

He raised his eyebrows, interest in his eyes. "And what would that be?"

"Grilled steak with onions, mushrooms and peppers. Twice-baked potatoes."

"A woman after my own heart," he declaimed, hand over said organ. "Your mom told me you were a great cook."

"When?" she asked, sobering at the thought of her mother.

"I don't remember exactly." He shrugged. "It was several years ago, after you'd visited for a weekend."

She breathed easier. At times, she'd felt her mother would like to push her and Jeremy toward each other. That could be her imagination, but the idea made her uncomfortable.

"Ready?" he asked.

"Yes." She stuck her wallet in her pocket, grabbed a floppy sun hat and followed him out. "The sheets," she said. "I forgot to put them in the dryer."

"We'll get them when we get back." He led the way to the truck. After they were a few miles down the road, he said, "You don't like it when your mother talks about you. Why is that?"

"My mother's job is to herd people together into family units," she explained, deciding on candor since he'd been open with her that morning. She flashed him a wry smile. "Since she thought I didn't do very well on my own, I've often felt she was trying to guide me—gently, of course— toward those she sees as good possibilities."

"And that's why you're so standoffish when you visit?"

She hesitated. "Well, I guess you could put it that way."

"I'm sorry," he said at once. "I didn't mean—"

"That's okay. I do tend to clam up when I feel pushed."

At the double-S curve, Jeremy parked in a pullout area. They walked up the highway, careful of the busy summer traffic heading into or out of the dinosaur park.

Evidence of past work was visible in the terracing of the steep slopes above the highway. When she asked about the problems with the area, he found himself explaining road construction much more than he usually would to an outsider.

But then, she seemed much more interested than the average person, asking questions that showed surprising understanding.

"So by cutting the terraces into a slant toward the hill and directing the runoff toward the culvert, using rocks to slow the water, you can halt erosion?"

"Usually. When we get a really hard rain after a period of drought, the land just won't soak up the moisture fast enough. The runoff can be fierce and take a lot of soil with it."

"Hmm, that probably wreaks havoc with your landscaping."

He studied her for a second. "You seem to be catching on to our problems pretty fast."

She laughed, and he was fascinated by the sound.

"I've been listening to Marti and the crew. During breaks, I read your reports. You made the situations very clear."

"One has to speak in simple words to the bottom-line boys," he told her ruefully.

"Speaking of which, are we done with the audit?"

"I wish. Someone from the state accounting office will be in next week, I think."

"You have as many regulations and rules to follow

as we do in the education programs. I've often wondered if anyone ever reads the reports I send in."

"I know what you mean."

After climbing over the slopes, he wrote down the items he needed to discuss with Gordan. He also had to find stabilizing fence to place over the area above the original terrace.

"There's no budget to buy it," he told her, "so I'm trying to find leftover fencing somewhere in the state."

"Is the fence to keep deer off the road?" she asked, glancing up the very steep slope at the ridge of the hill.

He shook his head. "It's laid directly on very fractured rocky ground to help keep everything in place, especially during severe storms."

"Oh, I've seen those before. In California, next to a job site my father was working on."

They smiled at each other in understanding. It was one of those perfect moments when mind meets mind, she thought as they carefully made their way down the treacherous incline, a sort of bond...no, nothing so deep as that, but a shared moment....

Later, he stopped at the barbecue place, a hole-in-the-wall restaurant that catered to hungry tourists sightseeing in the national park.

"Have you seen the dinosaur digs?" Jeremy asked.

"Not in person. I saw a special on the area on TV a few years ago."

"We'll go over one day. I have a friend who works there. He loves to show people around and expound on the latest theories."

"Like dinosaurs were warm-blooded critters and birds are their direct descendents?"

"Yeah, things like that."

He gave her a keen glance as if questioning how she knew that. "I read a lot," she answered the silent question.

"Rather than date?" He grimaced. "Ignore that," he requested and took a big bite of the delicious barbecue sandwich.

She glanced around the crowded dining room, catching many glances on them. When she looked outside, she saw her and Jeremy's reflections in the windowpane.

She studied the images as if she were one of the other diners. They were a striking couple—both tall, their contrast in coloring complementing each other.

Sunshine and shadow, he'd described them.

Smiling, she realized she did feel bright and sunny today, all the way through to her soul.

After lunch, they returned to the cabin. Zia put the sheets in to dry, then settled on the sofa with a novel while Jeremy relaxed in a recliner and watched a ball game on TV.

All they needed, she thought sardonically, was a dog on the hearth rug, and the cabin would be a picture of family bliss.

And children? Did she envision those, too?

Chapter Nine

Zia circled every possible rental in the Sunday paper and spent every spare moment of the following week looking at the choices. She found one place she liked, two rooms in the home of a widow. While it had its own entrance and the privacy she felt was necessary, it also came fully furnished.

Her furniture would have to stay at Jeremy's place, which she didn't think fair, or she would have to move it to a storage facility and pay a monthly fee. Not a good choice since she was counting her pennies these days.

A conviction that this move should never have taken place grew in her. While she couldn't go back to her old job and apartment, surely she could find something in Provo or Salt Lake City that would tide her over. She had good management and computer skills. Perhaps she should go into industry, where the pay was higher, rather than stay in the educational field.

However, some stubborn part of herself refused to give up on the local school system quite yet. She wanted children to have the best learning tools available. They needed all the advantages they could get during the growing years.

Putting the paper aside, she turned to more personal matters. Living in Jeremy's house was more difficult than she'd thought it would be. More intimate. More sexually charged, which was something she hadn't expected.

Although her friends had drooled over him, she'd never let herself think of him that way. However, she couldn't deny he was a potent package of masculinity—handsome, capable, kind, caring…so many things….

After the pleasant trip, they had both withdrawn, like turtles seeking the safety of their shells.

During the following week, they maintained a cordial surface friendliness, but there was a space between them that each was careful not to cross. The fact that he stayed late at work helped. She was often in her room by the time he came home from whatever site he'd been at that day.

On Thursday, he came in later than usual. He brought in three grocery bags, then returned to his truck for a case of beer.

That surprised her since she'd never seen him drink at home.

"There's a poker game tomorrow night," he told her,

storing the items in the kitchen. "It's my turn to have the guys over."

She nodded.

"We usually play past midnight," he continued, giving her a thoughtful frown as if wondering what to do with her.

"I see. Should I spend the night at the inn?"

He hesitated, then shook his head. "I just wanted to give you fair warning. We sometimes get pretty noisy."

"Oh," she said, relieved. "No problem. I have a book I've been meaning to start. I'll stay in my room and read."

"Okay." He stored the beer in an ice chest. "Uh, you might not want to wear those pajamas. If you come out to the kitchen for something."

The sleepwear was a silky material, with pretty lace inserts near the hem of each sleeve and pant leg. The calf-length robe was a beautiful lace over a silk lining, which made the outfit opaque and quite modest, in her opinion.

"It was a gift from Krista for Christmas," she said, as if this somehow justified her wearing it.

"Yeah, well, it's…mmm." He finished the sentence with a sound that was a cross between a growl and an "ahem."

"It's provocative?" she asked, surprised.

"It's very…pretty."

She got the idea. "I can wear a pair of old sweats. Would that be okay?" She managed to keep the facetious note out of her voice and expression.

"Sure." He sounded relieved.

* * *

On Friday evening, after checking that she'd left nothing personal in any part of the house, other than her room, Zia prepared a meal of chicken salad on a big plate of greens with grapes and cherry tomatoes.

Jeremy set up a portable camping table in the sunroom and laid out bags of chips, then placed the beer in a large cooler next to the table. To her amazement, he turned a fire extinguisher on the beer, creating a fog of carbon dioxide in the cooler.

"I've never seen anyone do that."

"It's the fastest way to chill it," he said, dumping a bag of ice on top to maintain the temperature. "You have to recharge the extinguisher after you use it, though, so you shouldn't do it unless you have a spare."

"Do we?"

"Yes. This one is from under the bathroom sink. There's another larger one in the kitchen."

She'd seen the kitchen one, but she'd been careful not to invade the drawers and cabinets in other parts of the house.

Afraid of what she might find in a bachelor residence?

Ignoring the question, she took a glass of iced tea to her room, closed the door and settled down for an evening of reading. The novel was thick, but she figured she would finish it if the poker game lasted into the wee hours.

Shortly after seven-thirty, she heard the crunch of tires on the gravel drive. The men arrived as a group and came into the house, their voices jocular as they greeted each other.

Soon their steps sounded in the hall outside her door, then they went out the door leading to the sunroom. One man was telling a rafting story about taking his really dumb brother-in-law down the Green River.

The volume decreased suddenly as the door closed.

Yawning, she started to prop her feet on an ottoman when she realized someone—a stranger—was gazing in the window.

Startled, she nodded at the man, then with a casual smile, reached over and pulled the curtains closed. Since the poker table and snacks were at the other side of the large screened room, it hadn't occurred to her that anyone would peer in her window.

For some reason, the fact that the man had looked in on her, bothered her. She checked to make sure there wasn't a slit where the draperies met.

Like anyone cared what she was doing, she mocked her nervy state. The men were obviously having a great time on their own.

For the next three hours she read steadily—a novel about an orphan who was determined to make a name for herself in the corporate world and naturally made several enemies along the way, all of whom tried to hinder her rise to success.

Male guffaws greeted the end of some story one of the men had told, interrupting her concentration.

She laid the book aside, resting her head on the comfortable padding of the chair. Occasionally she could pick out Jeremy's baritone among the other voices.

When she did, her heart would give a little lurch of surprise, which startled her.

By midnight, the house had cooled down from the day's heat.

Zia sipped the last drop from her tea glass, then gazed at the door to the hall. She wondered how much longer the poker party would go on. First of all, she needed to go to the bathroom, and she wanted a cup of hot tea while she finished the novel.

Well, she wasn't a prisoner. There was no reason she couldn't slip out of her room, do her thing, then get back before anyone noticed. From the sounds of merriment in the sunroom, that shouldn't be difficult to do.

Wearing thick socks, she went to the door, peered out, saw the bathroom door was open and headed for it. In a couple of minutes, she again checked that the coast was clear, then headed for the kitchen.

A half-empty box of brownies from the local bakery sat on the counter. The smell of chocolate was irresistible. After heating a cup of water in the microwave oven and placing a bag of herbal tea in to steep, she poured half a glass of milk and placed it, along with a fat brownie, on a plate.

"Caught ya," a male voice said behind her.

She dropped the plate. Fortunately it was only an inch from the counter and didn't break. "You startled me," she said, adding a smile to soften the accusative tone. She really didn't like being sneaked up on.

He was the same man who'd looked in the window at her. If he'd been one of the crew from the bridge site, she would have felt less...less...uneasy about being blocked in the close quarters of the kitchen. The stranger positioned himself at the end of the island, filling the opening.

"So who are you?" he asked, his smile too broad, his manner too cordial. "Jeremy didn't tell us he had a...visitor."

She didn't like his suggestive tone. His eyes seemed to be looking right through her clothes, traveling over her body. His grin seemed predatory to her.

"I'm an old family friend," she said quickly. "I recently moved to this area. Jeremy has been kind enough to let me rent a room in his home until I can find a place of my own."

There, that should make everything clear.

The man moved closer. Zia stepped back until her hip was against the counter. "An old friend, huh? Lucky Jeremy."

His tone dropped in depth. His smile was broad and sort of loose-lipped. While he may have thought he was coming on as sexy as a movie star, she thought he was a bit full of himself and had had a tad too much beer, although the keenness of his gaze said he was far from inebriated.

When he moved closer, trapping her in the corner, she wasn't afraid. With three other men close by, she could always yell for help. However, that could lead to an awkward moment between them and their stupid friend.

She picked up the plate in one hand and the teacup with the other. "If you'll excuse me," she said, treading the line between friendly and frosty, "I'll head back to my room."

He didn't take the hint and move aside. Instead he pressed closer, so that she had to hold the plate right under her chin and against her chest to keep from touching him.

"Pretty little gal like you could stay for free at my place," he said, bending over and blasting her with alcoholic vapors.

He was a tall guy, taller than Jeremy and heavier, too. A ripple of annoyance and discomfort speared through her. She groaned silently. It had been a long time since she'd been in a situation where she had to dissuade a determined male. Here, in this house, she hadn't expected it.

"Be careful," she warned, giving him an innocent smile. "I don't want to spill this boiling hot tea on you."

That caused him to blink.

"Can't find the bathroom, Smitty?" Jeremy asked, stopping at the island and leaving enough room for the other man to get out of the kitchen.

"I found something better," Smitty replied, sending another wave of fumes into Zia's face.

She huffed. Loudly.

"I don't think the lady wants your attention," Jeremy continued in a calm, amused manner. "I've known her to freeze a polar bear into a dead stop at twenty paces."

This caused the poker friend to laugh. "I think I get the drift." He backed off. "You didn't mention a housemate."

"She's a guest," Jeremy said. This time his tone was firmer, darker, with a dangerous edge. "She isn't to be disturbed."

Smitty nodded and backed off a good three feet. "I didn't realize how things were between you two. Sorry, ol' man." He headed down the hall toward the back.

Zia took a relieved breath. "Thanks," she told Jeremy, "I was trying to decide whether to yell or throw the hot tea on him. You saved me from either."

He spun around and left.

Hearing the door close at the back of the house, she hustled to her room and not only closed the door but locked it, too.

Her appetite gone, she set the milk and brownie aside, then paced the floor, sipping the tea. At the window to the sunroom, she stopped and stared at the curtains, feeling unfairly judged.

Jeremy said something, a joke from the way the men laughed, Smitty's being one of the loudest chortles among the group.

Was it a joke at her expense? Or was she being too sensitive, or maybe egotistical? They probably weren't discussing her at all.

Moving away from the window, she resumed her seat and reminded herself that the world didn't revolve around her.

As if she hadn't learned that a long time ago?

She sighed, suddenly near tears for no good reason…except that she again felt like an outsider, the intruder who never quite fit in.

Oh, quit feeling sorry for yourself.

Picking up the book, she propped her feet on the ottoman and read for another hour. Finished with the story, she flicked out the light and sat in the dark, unwilling to go to bed while the strangers were in the house.

The odd restlessness returned, stronger this time.

Shortly after one, the game broke up. Ten minutes after that, the place was silent as the hum from the last vehicle to leave faded into the distance. Straining her ears, she tried to figure out what Jeremy was doing, but couldn't hear a sound.

Then, "You can come out now," he said from the other side of her door, nearly making her leap from the chair.

She flicked on the lamp, then opened the door.

His dark gaze took in her sweats, then the milk and brownie on the table next to the book and empty teacup. "That looks good. I think I'll have some before I hit the hay."

When he headed toward the kitchen, she followed, carrying the snack she hadn't eaten. She realized it had been hours since she'd had dinner and she really was hungry. The interlude in the kitchen had temporarily forced it from her mind, but now she felt safe again.

Safe? She meant relaxed. She was relaxed with the other men gone.

Jeremy was already seated at the island when she joined him there. He wolfed down two brownies and a large glass of milk.

"What was going on between you and Smitty?" he

asked, in a manner, or so she thought, that implied she'd lured the man there against his will.

"Nothing. He was surprised to find you had a house-guest. Apparently you hadn't told your friends. He said I could stay at his for free." She laughed briefly, cynically. "Nothing is ever free."

"Got it all figured out, do you?" he said in the same sardonic tone that she'd used.

She realized that, at nearly two in the morning, he seemed to be spoiling for a fight and that this wasn't a good time for any kind of discussion. She didn't need a repeat of last weekend and the eruption of passion between them. That idea was more unnerving than the tense moments with his poker buddy. She put her dishes in the sink.

However, there was one thing she wanted to make clear. "The incident with your friend wasn't my fault." She gestured to her clothing. "I'm not wearing anything remotely provocative—"

"You don't have to," he muttered. "You look good enough to eat in anything."

She gave him a frosty glare. "I didn't ask for his attention and I wasn't overly friendly. It wasn't my fault," she stated again in succinct tones, "and I'm not going to take the fall for some guy with a beer buzz. As if I'd be interested in someone like him."

"Yeah, you could do a lot better. Why haven't you?" he asked with a snarl.

"I'm going to bed," she said, furious with him and the whole male population. "Good night."

He caught her arm, causing her to turn toward him as she walked past. "Don't let me run you off. I'm being an SOB. Sorry. I guess it's the late hour and…and other things."

Their eyes locked and questions flickered between them. A tremor started deep inside her and disrupted her thinking. Tension arced between them, raw, primitive and powerful.

She wanted him, this man who was so many things that were good and trustworthy and dependable, things that had been missing in her life….

"Zia," he murmured on a ragged breath.

She closed her eyes, knowing she was lost to reason. His hands touched her waist as he stepped forward. Lifting her arms, she locked them around him and buried her face against his chest.

Sensation poured through her. She took in the scent of him, the fresh-as-all-outdoors aroma of his clothing, the woodsy smell of his aftershave and shampoo.

And there was the warmth. His lips on her neck. His arms surrounding her. His breath touching her cheek as he moved upward and over her face. Deep down inside her, in a central place that had been protected by an icy barrier for a long, long time, a fire started, scaring her even as it consumed her.

"Come to me," he whispered.

When he moved back enough to look into her face, she gazed up into eyes as dark and endless as midnight and nodded.

To her surprise, he swept her into his arms and

carried her down the hall. The journey took seconds, an eternity—past the laundry, the bathroom, her door and finally to his bedroom.

Inside, he set her on her feet beside the bed. With one easy movement, he swept the covers aside, then his hands settled at her waist. Shivers chased along her spine as need grew.

Jeremy wasn't surprised that his hands were trembling as he lifted the sweatshirt over her head and tossed it aside. The hunger was the greatest he'd ever known.

His body tightened convulsively as she stroked along his chest and ended at his jeans. Through the pound of blood in his head, he heard the rasp of the zipper as she pulled the tab downward. The material flapped open, revealing the hard thrust of his arousal against his briefs.

When she touched him more intimately, caressing in the gentlest of strokes, he sucked in a harsh breath as need and yearning and red-hot passion flowed through his veins.

It was torture and delight, pain and pleasure, intensity, ecstasy, everything he'd ever read or thought desire could be.

With her. This woman. Only this one.

Zia pushed impatiently at the layers of clothing. She wanted nothing between them, nothing but the sweet, fierce need that surged through her. And him.

"Okay," he murmured, as if reading her mind.

With quick movements, the rest of their clothing was disposed of, falling to the floor in a heap around them. Then he lifted her once more and laid her on the big, comfortable bed.

Again his scent engulfed her as she inhaled deeply.

"Jeremy," she whispered. "I've wanted this…for a long time, I think. But I didn't know it."

He lay beside her, his body half over hers, his hand sliding through her hair as he spread it over the pillow. "It's odd to finally admit it," he agreed. "As if we're giving away a deep, dark secret that, once disclosed, can't be hidden again."

She cupped his cheek and gazed into his eyes. "Perhaps it should stay hidden."

When he shook his head, she was relieved. She didn't want to suppress the hunger that seemed to fill all the empty places inside her. For once she felt whole.

He smiled at her then, and it was magic. It healed the tiny, achy cracks in her heart.

When he caressed down her body, the pleasure in his touch overcame all else. Like meteors filling a starry sky, spirals of delight shot through her. She sighed and moved against him, opening herself, inviting his touch.

Jeremy wanted time to savor, to enjoy each second, but his body's demand was for quick, raw sex. When she moved against him, he felt her impatience and realized it matched his own.

He glided his fingertips over the lush smoothness of her abdomen and onto her thighs, then into the moist cleft as she thrashed her legs in restless invitation. She said his name with a little catch in her throat.

It was the sexiest sound he'd ever heard.

Lowering his head, he took her lips in a thousand kisses, each one a separate and special treasure. Tongue met tongue, engaged in a playful duel. He took in her taste, her spicy scent, the feel of his skin on hers.

And there was more.

He kissed her perfect breasts, felt her lift to him in the sweetest welcome he'd ever known. His heart beat so hard it felt as if it might leap out of his chest. Circling her navel, he found the stud gone and was glad he didn't have to be careful of it, although looking at it flash as she'd danced last week had been alluring and arousing.

When he dipped lower, he heard her gasp and then moan as desire built. He pressed his face against the sweet-smelling Venus mound, then flicked his tongue over the moist folds of her body.

Her hands stroked his head, then clenched in his hair as her breathing quickened.

He laughed softly and spent another eternity driving her to the brink, then pulling back just enough to bring her down a bit.

But there came a point when that wasn't enough for either of them. Panting, he rolled away and grabbed a condom from the bedside drawer.

"Let me," she requested.

When she took it from him and slid it home, he thought he was going to lose it right then.

"Now," she told him, urging him into place.

Grasping at control, he slid between her thighs and found the welcome he wanted. With one easy push from him, with one upward thrust from her, they came together in blissful unison.

"Wait," he said when she moved against him.

She gave a tiny sound of protest, but she stilled the sexy movements that nearly drove him out of his mind. Only her hands continued caressing him, along his back, his sides, over his hips and down his thighs. When she slipped a hand between them and gently massaged, he hissed out a harsh breath as his control seesawed precariously.

"Too close to the edge," he warned.

She snuggled against him, rocking her hips a little. "Me, too," she told him, kissing his throat and following his collarbone to his shoulder. She bit him playfully and tilted her hips a bit more.

"Ahh," he groaned.

Zia knew she couldn't hold out another second when he caressed her with full strokes of his body against hers, sliding over the pubic mound, then down again, building sensation on sensation until everything disappeared but where they touched.

"Yes," she moaned, a plea for completion. "Oh, yes."

Jeremy felt her spasm around him, felt the slam of air in and out of his lungs, then the wild surge as release came in wave after wave of intense pleasure. He spent himself inside her, feeling the bliss spread like warm honey to every part of his body and even into his mind...his soul....

At some point, he heard her take a deep, shaky breath and let it out slowly, as if she were utterly weary. As gently as possible, he rolled them to the side and laid one leg over her thigh, holding the bond between their bodies as long as possible.

Her eyes were closed, and her lovely face glowed

with a sheen of perspiration. He brushed the curling tendrils from her face and kissed her brow, her temple, unable to stop touching her.

For the first time in his life that he could recall, his body had gone beyond the command of his mind. Odd, but he didn't feel a need for caution, as he usually did when a relationship threatened to become too intense. Instead, a welter of emotions coursed through him. He tried to sort them out.

Tenderness?

Yeah.

Wonder?

That, too.

Confusion?

Definitely.

Chapter Ten

Zia woke late on Saturday morning. She was alone in the big bed. The night had been wonderful, intense, fulfilling.

Foolish? Yeah, that, too.

Turning over, she clasped her arms around Jeremy's pillow and inhaled deeply. His scent filled her lungs while her heart filled with the wildest images. A man and woman. A crackling fire. Quiet, contented days of building a home together. A family.

Okay, feet back on the ground. The sun was up, and reality was staring her in the face. The truth was the attraction had been there for a long time. The wedding had been the catalyst that had forced her to recognize it. Everything that had happened since had reinforced it. For Jeremy, too, she thought.

So, what now? She wasn't sure, but one thing she knew: Jeremy didn't skip out if things got tough. He'd proven that more than once in the years she'd known him.

Rising, she pulled on the sweats, now neatly folded and laid on a chair. Had Jeremy said he was going to work today?

She couldn't recall.

There had been so many other things to think about…or not think about. She smiled wryly.

Blood rushed in a torrent through her veins as she remembered the insanity of the night. Actually, the wee hours of the morning. She had no idea of the hour they had finally gone to sleep, but she felt rested. And content.

After finding her socks and pulling them on, she went into the kitchen. The coffee was ready. She poured a cup and glanced outside. Jeremy's SUV was gone. A note on the fridge caught her eye. He would be out most of the day, she read, and maybe into the evening. A *J* for his signature. That was it.

Ah, the difficult "morning after." Did he really have to work, or would he rather not face her?

She studied the neat writing, the block printing of the capital letters that indicated an orderly mind, or so she'd once read. With a squeeze of her fist, she crumpled the paper, then tossed it in the trash.

After eating, she spent an hour cleaning the house and washing sheets and towels. Jeremy had already straightened up the sunroom and kitchen, removing all traces of the poker game.

Later, she took a long walk along the ridge trail

behind the house and found a shelter, a one-room log cabin, for lost or storm-stranded hikers. When she returned to the cottage, it was still empty.

The birdcalls in the trees, contrasted to the silence inside, seemed like the loneliest sound she'd ever heard.

Well, it wasn't as if she'd expected hearts and flowers or any sentimental stuff. Jeremy, protective and caring by nature, had come to her aid when she'd needed it, just as he had that night long ago when she'd been desperate and alone. The resulting tension had quite naturally escalated into passion. She didn't expect more.

Which was a good thing. The note had made it clear he wasn't offering declarations of undying love. She sighed, then smiled slightly. Life, she thought, was a complicated affair.

Glancing at the clock, she realized it was time to prepare dinner. That, at least, was one thing she was good at. She managed a laugh. Perhaps she should have been a famous chef.

Jeremy returned home just as the sky was turning from twilight to dark. He and Gordan had spent the day using a crane to load up the heavy fence used to stabilize slopes and had taken it to the double-S curve site in a dump truck. They would have to bring a crane to the site to lift it into place on Monday.

Pulling into the carport, his pulse sped up upon catching sight of Zia in the kitchen. He wondered if she'd prepared a meal for them. He was late. Would she be angry?

He entered the side door like a warrior expecting a

hidden land mine. To his amazement, she glanced up with a smile.

"Oops, caught in the act. I was about to sneak one of those brownies you brought home."

"Help yourself," he told her, returning the smile while parts of him went soft and other parts became hard.

"There's homemade soup in the refrigerator, in case you haven't eaten."

"Sounds good. Thanks."

She poured a glass of milk and set it beside the brownie plate at the island.

Maybe he could have resisted if her manner had been cool or if her eyes had been shielded instead of guileless. Or if he hadn't inhaled deeply as he passed her, drawing in that special exotic scent he associated with her.

He stopped abruptly.

When she glanced up at him, he was lost. He laid his hands on her shoulders and bent toward her lips. "Are you okay with this?" he asked, hesitating.

"I don't know," she said with a candor he was coming to expect from her.

Closing his eyes, he let himself enjoy the welcoming kiss. Her hands settled at his waist, softly at first, then tightening as the kiss went deeper, harder, more demanding.

Some part of his brain whispered a warning, then a curse, just before the pound of his blood wiped out all thought. He groaned and pulled her closer, the need growing as passion shot through him with lightning speed.

"How did I ever think I could resist you?" he asked with a soft laugh as they came up for air.

She stiffened against him. Before he hardly realized she'd moved, she was out of his embrace and on the other side of the island. Her lovely face was as smooth as if carved into stone.

"Is that a problem?" she asked, her manner cool and aloof.

"I think we need to talk," he said. "About last night and just now. Tell me what offended you."

She shrugged.

He thought over what he'd said as desire had clouded his mind. "Was it because I said I couldn't resist you?"

Her eyes met his. He recognized the expression. It was the same as when they'd danced at Krista's wedding, the one that said she might be present physically, but she wasn't in spirit.

"You have to give me a clue," he continued after ten seconds. The silent treatment was getting to him.

"It was a mistake to move here," she stated. "I knew there was an attraction—"

"Before that night at the motel in Boise?" he interrupted, surprised and irritated that she'd apparently known the hunger was there all this time and had fooled him into thinking she didn't.

She gazed out the window. So did he. He saw the erratic path of a firefly at the edge of the woods. His life seemed to be following the same unpredictable pattern.

"At the wedding," she murmured, barely audible. "You stared when I came down the aisle. The dress Krista chose for me, the dance, the romantic atmosphere, that's when the attraction started. I think."

She laughed and it sounded hollow and lonely to him. A sudden pelting of his heart by the tiny darts of his conscience warned him about something, something important in their dealings, but he wasn't sure what it was.

"You were beautiful at the wedding," he murmured, "but I think there's more between us than that, and has been for a long time, maybe for years."

Her sardonic manner threw him off balance. "This summer has been a time of rather large changes in our lives. That fact, along with living in the same house, working together and sharing job problems, all add up."

"To passion?"

"Yes. Maybe we shouldn't take it all so seriously."

With a shrug, she picked up the brownie and bit into it, an act that sent a shaft of hunger spearing through him. Turning from her nonchalant attitude—the subject was closed, it appeared—he found the container of soup and heated a bowlful in the microwave.

When he took his place at the island, she finished her treat, put the used dishes away, then headed for her room.

"Wait," he requested. When she paused, he continued, "Gordan is having a picnic and ball game at his house tomorrow. Most of the work crew will be there. We're invited. Marti is cohosting and asked if we would come early and help."

The hesitation disappeared from her face when he mentioned the other woman. She nodded. "That sounds like fun. What time are we expected?"

"Around four."

"Great. That'll give me time to check out the Sunday ads."

"There's no rush on moving," he said, disturbed that she obviously wanted to leave and equally so that he didn't want her to go. "In spite of last night, there are no strings attached to your staying here."

"I know that, but it's probably best that I find my own place as soon as possible. Before things between us get any more out of control."

He could vouch for that. He wanted her *now,* in his arms, in his bed....

She walked away. In a moment, he heard the door to her room close softly but firmly, shutting out him and the passion. He snorted and shook his head. Passion wasn't only a pack of trouble, it was damn confusing, too.

He scarfed down the delicious soup, filled the bowl again, then stared at the steaming surface.

What he needed was to talk to someone who could help him sort through the situation. Uncle Jeff was out, due to being married to Zia's mom. His uncle would probably be horrified at their involvement.

Funny, but Zia was the only person who came to mind for a logical discussion. She might be distant at times, but he could speak openly with her.

Tired, he went to bed, noting that the sheets had been changed and no trace of her scent lingered. He missed her, he realized. One night, and he missed her being there with him, their bodies spooned together the whole night through.

* * *

A thunderstorm rolled through the mountains that night, cooling the parched earth and leaving the air sparkling when he arose on Sunday morning.

Jeremy went to town for the paper while Zia prepared blueberry pancakes. Returning to the cozy house, he had to admit to a lurch in the vicinity of his heart as he hurried inside.

After a mostly silent breakfast, he left her in the sunroom circling ads while he continued to clear brush in a hundred-foot radius around the house for fire protection.

At three, he took a shower and shaved, then reminded Zia it would soon be time to leave for the picnic.

She looked at her watch in surprise and put away her cell phone. When he'd come in for a drink during the afternoon, he'd heard her on the phone asking about apartments. Later, he'd heard her talking to her mother about the difficulty of finding an affordable place that was quiet and didn't remind her of a college boarding house.

The tension in his body each time he came into the kitchen was annoying. A man controlled his impulses, his uncle had told him on his eighteenth birthday.

Okay, he could do that, but that didn't mean he didn't have them to contend with. He heaved a heartfelt sigh.

He went out to the SUV and waited while she gathered her purse and a denim jacket. When she was belted in, he took off for Gordan's place, glad to be away from the cottage, which now seemed too small for the two of them, and relieved at the thought of mingling with a friendly crowd.

Yep, there was definitely safety in numbers.

* * *

Zia liked Gordan's home. It was a two-story frame house with living quarters downstairs and bedrooms upstairs, similar to the one she and her mother had lived in during her school years. It was over eighty years old, he told her, giving her a brief tour.

Marti was in the kitchen. She gave Zia a hug and set her to work slicing tomatoes for the hamburgers the men would cook outside on the grill. When a boy and a girl came in requesting snacks, she introduced her children. "Troy will be a seventh grader and Jillian will be in the fifth when school starts."

"Have you met any of the kids you'll be going to school with?" Zia asked.

"Sure," Troy told her. "At day camp."

After they rushed back outside, Marti told her about the day camp at the community center. "They have sports and learning programs, also tutoring for those who need extra help."

"That's really great." Zia felt a pang that the curriculum program wasn't going to be integrated with the overall educational system. Her temporary job would be to set up the computer accounting program and teach someone else to use it.

"Ah, here's Tina and her family," Marti said.

The site secretary carried a diaper bag while her husband brought the sleeping baby inside in a portable car seat for infants. She introduced her husband, Richard Zayres, who said hello and headed outside to join the men.

Anderson, the baby, was darling, Zia thought, gazing at the tiny features. The couple had given him a hyphenated last name, Ramsey-Zayres, Tina explained. He'd weighed five and a half pounds at birth, but he was gaining rapidly.

"He sleeps through anything," Tina told the other two women, "and is growing like mad. I didn't know something so little could eat so much."

Zia listened while Marti and Tina discussed formula and baby food. Since she had no experience with either, she kept silent.

For the next hour, the three women worked companionably. They made potato and macaroni salads, baked cookies and a huge pan of gingerbread, and greeted other families as they arrived.

Soon there was a volleyball game in progress in the side yard, as well as a game of horseshoes. Marti's son, a natural leader, organized races among the younger crowd.

Some of the men had brought folding tables and chairs. These were set up under some shade trees beside a long picnic table. A baseball diamond had been marked off in a clearing beyond the eating area.

The easy chatter and laughter reminded Zia of Jeremy's family and their enthusiasm for each other's news at gatherings.

Marti kept her busy in the kitchen, then they set the food on long tables on the patio so the guests could help themselves. Zia felt useful and happy. Working with the women, she didn't have to be on guard against unwelcome and unwanted advances.

It came to her that she was comfortable at the work site, too. The crew worked well together and treated each other with respect. No one came on to her or acted as if she were other than one of them.

The tone of the workplace was usually set by the boss, she mused. Jeremy was a good manager, fair-minded and hardworking, expecting the same from himself as he expected from the crew, serious when it came to problems but able to take a joke.

Placing a giant bowl of chips on the patio table, she caught his gaze on her. On an impulse she couldn't resist, she made a face at him by crossing her eyes and scrunching her nose.

Then she laughed at his surprise.

Gordan and Steve, the site engineer, saw her and laughed, too. Steve, Zia noted, was with Sadie, the flag girl. The young woman was pretty and vivacious as she flirted with the men in an innocent manner that was somehow endearing.

Zia wondered how she did it.

She glanced down at her light blue slacks and white top imprinted with blue and yellow flowers, the sandals that disclosed her pink toenails. Like Sadie, most of the women wore shorts with running shoes, except for Marti and a couple of older women, who also wore pants. Surely no one would consider her outfit provocative, but then her sweats hadn't seemed that way, either.

"Okay," Gordan called out shortly before six, "come and get it while the burgers are hot."

Soon people swarmed around the food tables. Zia

made sure the bowls stayed supplied until everyone had filled a plate.

"Our turn," Marti said, grabbing two glasses of iced tea and handing one to her.

Zia went down the food line behind her friend. When their plates were full, a familiar voice called out, "Over here."

Gordan and Jeremy had saved each of the women a place. Zia slid onto a bench beside Jeremy while Marti sat opposite her beside Gordan. Steve, Sadie, Tina and Richard were also there.

Zia was acutely aware of Jeremy's hip against hers.

"We missed you guys at Beaver's Friday night," Sadie said. "The band was a new one and really good."

"What happened to the old band?" Marti asked.

"They've moved on to Salt Lake City."

"Oh, yeah, the big time," Gordan added, drawing chuckles from the others.

Zia listened to the flow of conversation as contentment filled her. She wondered why she felt at ease with this group, why it seemed as if they accepted her for herself and she didn't have to be on guard with them.

When Jeremy stirred beside her, she glanced at him. His smile seemed natural and relaxed. She smiled back, feeling that they had gotten past the hurdle of the previous night and were on friendly terms again. That was a relief.

When Anderson woke from his nap, Tina brought him outside. She'd prepared a bottle for him.

"Oh, may I feed him?" Zia asked, finished with her meal and seeing that Tina wasn't. "Will he let me?"

"He'd love it," Tina assured her.

She placed the baby in Zia's lap, tested the warmth of the formula and handed the bottle to Zia.

Zia laughed softly as the tiny rosebud mouth closed around the nipple and sucked hungrily. Her own nipples contracted unexpectedly, which rather surprised her.

Jeremy turned toward her. "Lean on me," he advised.

As if they'd done this a hundred times, she leaned into his side, aware of his arm behind her. She gave him a grateful glance, then concentrated on little Anderson as he ate with noisy delight.

The baby stopped once and gave her a milky smile, then continued the meal. Halfway through the bottle, Tina told her to burp him. Zia put the child to her shoulder and patted his back. He waved his fists in the air, clearly annoyed.

Jeremy placed a pad on her shoulder. "In case he spits up," he said.

"Oh." Zia shot him a questioning look. "You seem to know a lot about babies."

"Not really, but I recall being around Krista when she was young. And I've observed friends with their families." He nodded toward Tina and Richard.

"Now we know who to call on when we need a sitter," Tina declared.

Zia gazed into the baby's blue eyes while he ate. He gazed back as if enraptured with her. A knot of emotion formed in her throat. He was so tiny, so perfect, so trusting that life would be good to him.

Her heart squeezed into a tight ball, and her eyes burned. She fervently prayed that all his dreams would come true.

As if looking back on someone she'd known long ago, she saw herself as she'd been as a child, confidently expecting the best from life. It had been a terrible shock when her father had moved out. She'd been frightened. She'd thought she'd done something wrong. When her mom had explained she hadn't, that grown-ups sometimes found they couldn't get along, she'd thought it must be Caileen's fault that her fun, laughing father had gone away.

Sammy, the love of her young life, had been another of life's great disappointments. She'd loved him with all the fire and passion of her teenage heart, but he'd walked...practically run...to the nearest exit when she'd needed him the most.

She'd locked away her dreams after that.

Now, looking into Anderson's trusting gaze, she realized children came into the world expecting nurture and other things, such as fairness, kindness and trustworthiness, from those close to them.

"And honesty. You have a right to that, too," she murmured to the child. He smiled once more before closing his eyes and going to sleep in her arms, trusting her to keep his world secure while he slept.

She silently forgave the child she'd once been for wanting more from those she'd loved than they could apparently give.

Laughter brought her attention to the area beyond

the lawn. Two teams had been formed with Gordan heading one and Marti the other. Zia watched as Jeremy stripped out of his shirt and tossed it over a low branch on a tree. Marti named him the pitcher for their team as they took the field.

While she'd seen Jeremy play tag with his cousins or sandlot ball with their friends, plus those brief moments at the local town park, she'd never seen him in this type of setting. His teammates obviously valued him as a good player.

After two hits and three strikeouts, Gordan's team lost their turn at bat. Marti's team was now at the plate. One of the young single women, the date of a forklift operator, swung a bat to loosen up, then took her position facing the pitcher.

Other than basketball and soccer, Zia didn't have much experience at playing games. Since leaving school, she hadn't had an opportunity to engage in any sports, other than solitary jogging. When the other woman got a base hit, Zia was envious of her skill as Jeremy and the team cheered her on to second base.

Jeremy came over and sat beside her. He drank down half a glass of tea, then poured another.

Zia inhaled the scent of his heated body as if it were a magic elixir. Longing rose to her throat, making her breathless and light-headed. She carefully laid Anderson in the infant seat on the bench beside her. He slept blissfully on.

When she straightened, she found Jeremy's eyes on her, his expression somewhat puzzled, as if she were an enigma he was trying to figure out. "What?" she finally asked after he took another long drink of tea.

"Toni was surprised you were an only child," he murmured. "She said you were a natural with children."

Other people had said the same thing at various times during her career. However, children did seem to trust her. Or maybe it was that she trusted them, she admitted, and that was why she felt a rapport with her youngsters.

"I've worked with kids in education programs for years," she explained. "I like them. Unlike a lot of adults, they're eager to try new things and learn different skills. It doesn't even matter if it's hard work, as long as it's interesting or challenges them in some way."

When she gave him a quick smile, he reached out and tucked a strand of hair behind her ear, his manner solemn. "Sometimes it takes adults longer to recognize a good thing when it comes along, doesn't it?"

The introspection in his tone sent a shiver down her back as she wondered what he was thinking. "Sometimes," she agreed.

"Jeremy, you're at bat," Marti called.

He touched her again, a light pat on the shoulder, then left to take his place at the plate.

She stared at the smooth ripple of muscle across his shoulders as he lifted the bat into position and shifted his weight to put power into his swing.

Memories of their night together returned. She knew his touch, the feel of his body against hers. She'd run her hands over his back, had felt the strength of his thighs between hers. She knew his gentleness, his pleasure in pleasing her, his sweet kisses in the after-glow as he'd tucked her into the curve of his body and settled them into sleep.

A warm, melting sensation ran over her, making her glad to be sitting down.

Like a flash of lightning over King's Peak, it hit her that she felt more than casual attraction for Jeremy, that the night had been more than great sex for her.

Love?

No, not that, she denied the emotion as the pitcher for the other team arched his arm back for the throw. Jeremy's whole body tensed, then moved in a perfectly timed sequence as the ball sped toward him. She wasn't at all surprised when he hit a home run. Or that the ball seemed to fly straight toward her heart.

She instinctively ducked.

Zia was glad when Jeremy pulled under the roof of the carport shortly before ten that evening. They'd for-gotten to leave a light on, so the cottage was dark, but it nevertheless seemed welcoming.

However, there was really no refuge from the knowl-edge that lurked in her heart. Falling for Jeremy was the most foolish thing she'd done in a long time.

"I'm beat," he said when they were in the house. He flipped on the kitchen light, then yawned and stretched.

His T-shirt rode up his lean torso, revealing a sliver of flesh above his jeans. Hunger for something besides food pinged through her. "You had a busy weekend."

"Yeah. Did you enjoy today?" He gave her a

probing glance as if assessing the possibility of her telling him the truth.

Her answer was sincere and enthusiastic. "Oh, yes. It was fun." And it would be even better if he kissed her, if they spent the night in his bed.

Risking another quick look at his face, she detected nothing in the depths of his eyes. Apparently she was the only one who was about to fly apart. That seemed a good reason to head for her room. She started that way.

"Zia?"

She came to an abrupt halt as if hitting a glass wall. "Yes?"

"It was good of you to take care of the baby for Tina."

She nodded in acknowledgment of the compliment. "New parents need a break." She sounded as if she knew all about it. "Or so my mom always says."

"Marti was impressed, too."

Zia hoped the other woman wasn't going into matchmaking mode. "Do you think she and Gordan have a thing going?" she asked, glad to direct the conversation to someone else.

"Maybe," he said. A frown creased two tiny lines over his nose. "Marti seems to think we do."

"Uh, this probably isn't a good time to discuss a personal situation." She maintained a droll expression as she gave a playful warning. "Remember where it led Friday night?"

"How could I forget?" he questioned on a softer, gentler note that brought a rush of turmoil to her insides.

"It was foolish—"

"But good," he interrupted on a harder note. "So damn good."

"Yes," she agreed in total honesty. "Today, watching you play ball…" She stopped, unwilling to tell him how much she'd wanted to rub her hands all over his bare torso and soak up his warmth.

"Yeah, it was the same for me. You were quiet today, but not in a remote way as if you would rather be anywhere but there." He tilted his head slightly and studied her intently. "That's the way you seemed at the wedding."

"I know. That was because Lance and Krista were so happy and I was so envious." She shrugged helplessly. "I felt small and mean-spirited. I don't even believe in 'happily ever after' and yet I wanted…I wanted what they had."

Electric arcs seemed to flow between them as they stared at each other. She knew she should flee, that the moment was much too tempting after the passion they'd shared.

His shrug was cynical. "Don't we all?" he muttered, turning to snap the lock on the door before going behind the island to grab a brownie. "There's one more," he said. "You want it?"

She shook her head. "Are you going out to the work site in the morning?"

"No, I have meetings all day in town."

"Then I'll see you tomorrow night."

"Probably not. I'll be working a lot of hours while I check on several projects. This is one of the largest districts in the state, so I may not get back to town at all. I sometimes sleep on site."

"Well, then, I'll see you...whenever."

"Yeah," he said without looking at her.

Going to her room, she reminded herself that the demands of work were legitimate reasons for not coming home.

Chapter Eleven

On Monday, Zia started her dual employment, working at the bridge site in the mornings, then at the education department in the afternoons. During her lunch hour and in the early evening, she looked for a place to live, but nothing suited.

Jim Ramsey took her to see a charming house on a corner in town and only three blocks from her work. It was a delight—two bedrooms, two baths, a large kitchen and, best of all, a charming yard with tons of flowers and a patio with an old-fashioned swing. It was also for sale at a price she wouldn't consider even if she were looking to buy.

Finding an apartment had never seemed so difficult. During restless nights, alone in her bed and unable to sleep until Jeremy came in, she acknowledged this move wasn't going to work out. It wasn't going to be a new beginning that would lead to a wonderful life. This place wasn't going to be "home."

Wednesday, after spending the previous two afternoons installing the accounting program and checking its performance, she was ready to start training those who would be using it, with the department secretary first of all.

Brandy Cummings, a woman who looked as old as a desert cedar and whose name didn't seem to fit her at all, was barely five feet tall. Standing or sitting, Zia felt like a giant whenever she was around the other woman.

"This accounting system was approved by the federal Department of Education," she explained, both of them sitting in front of the computer terminal. "It *has* to be used for the financial reports."

"I understand," the secretary assured her. "Aren't computers wonderful? They have made our lives so much easier. You probably don't remember when we used carbon paper to make copies of letters, but I do. What a pain," she concluded in a droll manner.

Zia perused the older woman in surprise. Maybe this wouldn't be a lesson in futility, after all. Brandy seemed ready to tackle the job with enthusiasm. When Zia gave her a delighted grin, the secretary smiled back, then proceeded to pull up the file and, with a few questions, typed in the invoices that Zia had chosen to start the lesson.

At five, while they were closing up the office, Zia told her, "You did really great. I was much slower at catching on to the account setup and at inputting the data."

"Well, I had you to guide me," Brandy said with calm practicality, which Zia recognized was her trademark manner of conducting business. "And I have a secret weapon."

"Like what?" Zia asked curiously.

"My grandson. He spends part of each summer with me. He helped me set up a home computer so we could keep in touch by e-mail. Then, when I was having trouble balancing my checking account, we decided to try a personal finance program. Now all my bills are paid automatically and I download the bank info so that my account is balanced each month by computer. Josh and I play video games every evening when he visits, so I'm used to different types of programs."

"That's really super," Zia said, totally impressed.

That evening, after eating a salad in the sunroom and watching the changing colors of the sunset, she called her mother.

"You remember the secretary I told you about?" she asked after they'd exchanged greetings.

"The one older than the hills?"

"Yes. She's cool." Zia told her about the grandson and the computer. "I did the same thing to her that I've often felt people do to me—judge by appearances. She's really nice and very much 'with it,' as I'm sure her grandson would say."

"Good. That should make your work much easier."

Zia took a deep breath. She wasn't sure confession was good for the soul, but she had something to get off her chest. "It also makes me feel guilty, which is the way

I feel when I think of how impatient I was with you when you tried to give me good advice all those years ago. I've wanted to apologize for a long time."

"It's all part of growing up," Caileen said sympathetically. "I was pretty sure we would get through it."

Zia laughed when her mother did. "At the hospital," she continued, "I was so glad you had Jeff. He's a wonderful person."

"I agree," Caileen said lightly, "when he's not being pigheaded and all that."

"I'm not pigheaded," Zia heard Jeff exclaim indignantly in the background.

"He came in from the shop and heard that last part," Caileen explained, her manner so affectionate it caused Zia's heart to clench in envy of the couple's camaraderie. "He's trying to finish a commissioned sculpture, so we're having a late supper."

"I'll let you go then. Take care. Give my love to Jeff."

"I will. Zia?"

"Yes?"

"You'll find someone special, too, someone just for you. I was glad when you accepted the new job. It got you out of a rut." Caileen hesitated, then added, "Things have a way of working out. You'll see."

Her mother's encouraging words echoed in Zia's mind the rest of the evening. She must have sounded way down in the dumps for Caileen to give her a pep talk.

She grimaced. Now her mom would worry about her, which added another brick to her load of guilt about misjudging people and not listening to her mom while growing up. Where, she wondered ruefully, did wisdom come from?

The ringing of the telephone was a welcome interruption.

When she picked up, no one was there. One of the computer-generated telemarketer calls, she surmised. She'd had a couple last week and at least one every night for the past few days. She always hung up before someone came on the line and tried to sell her something.

However, before she could do so this time, a very low, very guttural male voice inquired, "Are you alone?"

Annoyed, she slammed the receiver down. She would let the machine answer Jeremy's home phone from now on. If it was him or someone she needed to talk to, then she would take the call.

When the phone rang again, she ignored it. The machine picked up. There was a soft click on the line as the caller hung up.

"You look worried," Marti said, buttering a roll, then taking a big bite.

Zia glanced at her friend in surprise. "I didn't realize it was so obvious."

"Probably only to me. My husband used to complain that I could read him like a book and he could never get away with anything. I would always ask if he was trying to." She studied Zia for a few seconds. "So, what's happening?"

Zia shrugged. "Some phone calls that are annoying, that's all."

"Don't belittle your gut reaction. If something feels wrong, it usually is. Are you getting obscene calls?"

"Not exactly. Just this really low, sort of rough voice that asks if I'm alone if I forget and answer the phone. I've been letting the machine pick up most of the time, in which case he hangs up. If it's the same person."

"Let Jeremy answer from now on."

"The calls come around dusk. Jeremy doesn't get in until much later, usually after I'm in bed."

"When did the calls start?"

"Last week, for sure. Maybe the week before, but I didn't get suspicious then. I thought it was a telemarketer and hung up before he said anything."

"Do you think it's someone who knows you and Jeremy?"

"Someone who knows he's working until all hours during the summer season?" Zia questioned.

"Maybe," Marti said.

A chill speared through Zia. Smitty came to mind. While he was obnoxious and full of himself, still, he was Jeremy's friend. Surely he wouldn't pester her with calls.

"I can't imagine who," Zia began, then stopped. Having fewer reservations about people didn't mean having blind trust. "Well, I'm screening all calls. Most people give up after a few tries when they don't get the results they want."

"You should mention this to Jeremy," Marti advised.

Zia nodded. Like when? At midnight? She didn't think it wise to approach him at that hour. Her heart clenched at the thought of going to him and telling him she was afraid....

Would he think she was putting him on? Coming on to him?

Later, at the house that evening, she sat in the sunroom, alone as usual, and wondered how things got so complicated.

That was simple. Emotion. And passion.

They clouded the most innocent action, made her question her every move where Jeremy was concerned....

The phone rang.

She went into the living room and waited for the answering machine to pick up. A very hoarse voice whispered, "Are you alone?" Then the line went dead.

"Yes, and I'm going to stay that way," she said in a snarl to the unknown prankster. Hearing an engine, she dashed to the kitchen window in relief.

It wasn't Jeremy.

She saw a vehicle parked at the curve in the driveway, its taillights toward the house. As she watched, it disappeared from sight, heading toward the main road.

Fear, then anger rolled through her. If that was the caller, she wasn't going to be intimidated, she silently informed him.

Lightning flashed, then thunder crashed directly over the cottage. She nearly jumped out of her skin. So much for brave talk, she thought sardonically as she looked around for a weapon and decided a hefty piece of firewood would do.

When she went to bed, she kept her sweats on and the cell phone on the bedside table. Her sneakers, the kind with quick fasteners instead of shoestrings, were at the ready beside the bed. A rain jacket was on the chair.

She made sure the bedroom door was locked, also the window onto the sunroom, before falling into a fitful sleep.

When she woke to the ring of the phone, she heard Jeremy's voice in the living room.

"Hello?" Pause. "Hello?" Another pause. "Who the hell is this?" he demanded.

She heard him hang up none too gently. With a smile, she closed her eyes, curled into a comfortable position and didn't wake again until the clock radio blared the weather report.

"Heavy rain most of the day," the forecaster announced.

Zia struggled from the warm bed. It was Friday. Tomorrow, she promised herself, she would sleep as late as she wanted.

Jeremy stared out the SUV in disgust as rain blew in a sheet of blinding drops across the road.

"We're not going to be able to get equipment in here for about four days," Gordan said.

"Yeah, tell me something I don't know." He managed a smile to soften the words. His irritation wasn't directed at his site supervisor, but at the mountain storm that disrupted the work.

The lower terrace at the double-S curve, the one he'd planned to stabilize that week, had washed out during the night in spite of the fencing they'd secured to the uppermost slope.

Officials wanted the road repaired ASAP due to development of the natural gas reserves in the Uinta basin. The jobs and money would be a big boon for the state and county economy.

"We might have to cut a new road," Gordan said, sounding as low as Jeremy felt.

"No funds," Jeremy replied. He backed in a semicircle. "Let's get out of here before the whole hillside gives way."

Wind rocked the vehicle as he drove down the winding gravel road. Rain fell in torrents as if someone poured buckets of water on the earth. Even with a four-wheel drive, the going was slow and treacherous. The trip took two hours. At the next intersection, they put out warning cones and a sign that told travelers the road was closed ahead.

"Marti and I are going to Beaver's for dinner tonight. We thought we'd check out the new band," Gordan mentioned once they were back on a paved surface. "She wondered if you and Zia wanted to join us."

Jeremy shook his head. "I'll be writing up reports and refiguring the schedule until all hours."

"If you can come out later for the dancing, we'll be there," the other man told him.

"Maybe," he said. "If I get done in time."

The last thing he needed to end the week on a perfectly toxic note was to watch a bunch of men falling all over themselves to dance with Zia. He just wasn't up to the aggravation of looking after her. No matter what she said about taking care of herself, he didn't trust some of the strangers who came to the area looking for adventure, often leaving families at home.

Back in town, Jeremy returned to his office while Gordan switched to his pickup and headed for the Desolation Canyon site. At least the storm hadn't hit that far south, so work was now on schedule at the bridge. The revised schedule, he added.

Sitting at his desk and listening to messages on the answering machine, he wondered where the week had gone. Here it was, Friday, and he didn't feel as if he'd accomplished a damn thing all week.

Except think of Zia first thing when he woke up and the last thing before he went to sleep.

The invitation to Beaver's reminded him of the coral stud she'd worn in her belly button the other time they'd gone to the popular tavern. And that reminded him of the night she'd spent in his bed.

The problem was, she'd felt just right lying next to him. Her skin had been satin smooth, her body welcoming, her little cries of pleasure adding to his own. A thousand memories crowded into his inner vision. Zia back from a jog up the ridge. Zia in the kitchen, humming as she prepared a meal.

Who knew that she liked to cook?

Actually, he hadn't known very much about her at all before she'd moved to town, he realized. She didn't invite intimacy, as a rule. No wonder. Guys like Smitty couldn't help but flirt outrageously with a woman who looked like a goddess.

He didn't have a lot of room to gloat. He hadn't been able to resist, either.

"Horndog," he muttered as his body stood to attention.

It was impossible not to react to her angelic face and the sexy lines of her lithe body.

With a loud—and disgusted—snort, he concentrated on the never-ending paperwork and finally e-mailed his latest findings off around ten, just as the next storm front came through. A crash of thunder startled him and caused the windows to rattle throughout the old building.

He shut down the computer and closed up the office. The electricity clicked off before he reached the front door. The hallway went pitch-black. He muttered several curses.

Just one more bright note to end the week on, he thought as he trailed his hand along the wall as a guide to the door. The streetlights were also off. Going outside, he locked the main door in the flash from a lightning bolt and headed for the SUV at a run as thunder crashed over his head.

He put all thoughts of the repairs that would be needed on the mountain roads out of his mind. There would be more than a few mud slides. However, emergency money would come out of another account, so the funding wouldn't be as great a problem. But the schedule would be shot to hell. Again.

Driving to his house, he encountered water running across the road in two places. By midnight, the low places would be dangerous to cross. He called Gordan via cell phone and asked him to get someone out to set up flash flood warning signs.

"Will do," Gordan promised.

The sounds of merriment in the tavern could be heard

clearly in the background. "Sounds as if the place has a crowd tonight," he said.

"Yeah. You should be here. The new band is really good."

"Some other time." Jeremy told Gordan to be careful going home and rang off. He gave all his attention to the road on the rest of the trip as the wind whipped this way and that.

A rabbit ran across the pavement in front of him. When he hit the brakes, the SUV went into a skid. He steered in the direction the rear wheels took and recovered. It was a dangerous night for man or beast.

A light was on in the kitchen, Jeremy saw when he rounded the last curve in the driveway. Its soft glow seemed to warm a place in his heart—

The light winked out.

He blinked as if a shroud had fallen over his eyes. The electricity must have gone off at his place, too. Lightning lit up the sky in a zigzag pattern, temporarily blinding him. He slowed and stopped before he ran into something.

Thunder echoed from the ridge behind the cottage, so loud it was almost deafening. He muttered an expletive as he eased the SUV under the carport next to Zia's car. The wind blew raindrops against the back of the truck with a clattering sound.

Hail, he realized.

Another flash of lightning had him waiting until his eyes adjusted to the dark again before attempting to go inside. From the glove box, he removed a flashlight and headed into the house.

The dead bolt was on, which surprised him. Zia didn't usually lock it when he was out, but used only the button lock on the doorknob. He had to search his keys by touch to find the one that fitted the bolt.

The howl of the wind increased as he opened the door, as if it wanted to beat him into the house. From the back, he heard the slam of a door, whipped shut by the draft.

He cursed again. The racket was enough to wake the dead. However he didn't hear anything from Zia's room.

After he closed the kitchen door, the sudden silence as the wind slacked off was eerie. The hair stood up on the back of his neck when he heard another door slam at the back of the house.

In a rush now, he headed for the sunroom, the beam from the flashlight forming a cone of visibility in front of him, otherwise all was completely dark.

Zia's door was closed as usual. He listened intently but heard no sound inside. The sunroom door creaked as the wind picked up again. He went into the screened room. A flash of lightning froze the scene in his vision for a second.

No one appeared to be there, but the hair stood up on the back of his neck. He flicked the flashlight to Zia's bedroom window. The curtains were open and he could see her bed.

The covers lay to one side of the mattress as if tossed there in a hurry. Alarm speared through him. Where the hell was she?

Zia had decided not to wait until the intruder got very far into the house. Awakened by the sound of an engine, she'd listened intently while assuring herself it was Jeremy.

However, the person had taken a long time to open the kitchen door. He must have picked the lock, no matter that she'd made sure the dead bolt was secure. The slam of a door had her jumping out of bed, sliding her feet into her jogging shoes and silently escaping out the sunroom door in a flash.

The wind caught the screened door and slammed it behind her. She mumbled a curse as she struggled into her rain jacket and zipped it while running across the open area behind the house.

After the second mysterious call that evening, she'd decided she would sneak out the back and up the ridge to the snow cabin if anyone broke into the cottage. The cabin door was heavy and bearproof, with wooden bars and brackets to bolt the door.

Jeremy, considerate of others, would have called out to let her know he'd arrived when the door slammed.

Shielding her cell phone under the jacket hood, she tried to call 9-1-1, but only got static. The storm had disrupted service.

"Zia," a voice bellowed behind her.

She reached the trees at that moment and ducked behind one to peer at the house. A flashlight swung from side to side across the clearing. Lightning lit the area, limning the trees, the house and a tall figure standing on the flagstones outside the sunroom.

"Zia, it's okay," Jeremy called. "Come back to the house."

The flashlight cast a trail of light in her direction. She stepped from behind the pine and cautiously approached. "Turn the light off. You're blinding me."

He directed the beam to the ground in front of her.

"Jeremy?" she said, stopping ten feet away, aware of her quick breathing after the mad dash and the cold rain that soaked the legs of her sweatpants.

The light went to his face so she could see him clearly. "Yeah, it's me. I didn't mean to scare you."

"It wasn't your fault. I thought someone had broken into the house. I've been getting calls—"

"What kind of calls?" he demanded, ushering her inside the sunroom.

"Someone calls and asks if I'm alone." She balked at going in the house. "My shoes are soaked."

"Mine, too. Leave them out here."

They left their shoes and dripping jackets in the outer room and went into the house. Jeremy gave her a piercing once-over.

"You're shaking."

She crossed her arms over her chest and willed the tremors to stop. Feeling foolish for overreacting, she said, "The electricity went off, which causes my clock to buzz and start blinking. That woke me. Then I heard someone drive up. It took so long for you to get in the house, I thought…"

"You thought I was someone breaking in?"

"Yes."

"Were you going to hide out in the woods until the coast was clear?" he demanded.

"There's a snow cabin up the ridge. I was going to barricade myself in there and wait for help. Assuming I could get through on my cell phone," she added, trying for a humorous note and failing.

He muttered an expletive. "I should have called and let you know I was on my way home—"

At that moment, two things happened—the lights came on and the telephone rang. They stood in the hall as if frozen.

"Are you alone?" the voice asked in a whisper. A click indicated he'd hung up.

Jeremy strode into the living room, grabbed the phone and punched in a code. "He's got his number blocked," he told Zia, his face grim as he replaced the phone. "How many of these calls have you had?"

"A few."

"Enough to frighten you," he concluded. "We'll put a block on the line. If the calling number is locked out, the caller can't get through. I'll have Smitty put a trace on the number, too."

"Smitty?"

"Yeah, he's a detective with the county."

"I thought the caller might be him."

Jeremy groaned, then came to her and laid his hands on her shoulders. "He came on too strong, but I didn't realize he'd frightened you." He tilted her face upward so he could gaze into her eyes. "God, Zia, I'm sorry. Smitty doesn't realize his size alone would scare a gorilla. Really, he wouldn't hurt a fly."

She nodded and squirmed under his touch. The heat

from his hands radiated into her shoulders while her feet felt icy.

"We're getting the floor wet," she told him, looking down at their feet. His socks and hers were soaking up moisture as water dripped from their pant legs.

"It doesn't matter," he said, his voice low and strained.

She glanced at his eyes, then away. Electric currents danced through her. Awareness of his physical presence circled her like a protective embrace, shielding her from her earlier fears, which now seemed foolish. "I'm sorry I acted like a—a coward."

"You're not a coward." He cupped her face, shocking her with the need his touch produced. "I think you're brave, more so than I ever realized."

She shook her head.

"Yes," he said in a near whisper. He bent his head, his face no more than two inches from hers.

She licked her lips, knowing what was coming…knowing and not able to resist. She waited, her gaze locked with his, until with a low groan he enclosed her in his magic embrace that made the world go away.

Their lips touched, parted, touched again, then meshed as hunger overrode caution. "I've missed you," he said.

"I've missed you, too."

Other words were there, on the tip of her tongue, but she held them back, unwilling to admit to more than the desire of the moment. They moved as one, their arms wrapping tightly around each other until they were molded together.

It was several minutes before they came up for air.

"Let's get out of these wet clothes," he suggested, taking her hand and guiding them along the hall.

In his room, they stopped beside the big, comfortable bed and peeled out of shirts, damp pants and wet socks.

"My feet are freezing," she complained, but followed it with a little, breathless laugh as something like joy flooded her heart.

"Get in bed. I'll warm them for you."

He tucked her against the pillows and pulled the covers up, then sat beside her and slid his hands under the sheet. With the most marvelous caresses, he massaged her feet back to warmth.

"Anywhere else?" he asked, giving her a sexy grin. "I like rubbing you."

"My back?" she suggested.

With soft laughter, he rolled her to one side and ran his big, gentle hands all over her back, her hips, her thighs, up the front of her legs, her abdomen and finally cupped her breast in his hand as he curved his body to hers.

"Better?" He smoothed her hair aside and pressed little nibbling kisses along her neck.

"Much." She turned to him, their legs meshing in the most natural way as if they'd lain together like this a hundred times. "Now I'll do you."

She glided her palms over his chest, enjoying the varying textures of his body as she explored down...and down....

"Easy," he warned.

But she didn't want easy or slow. With a push, she shoved him on his back—with a little assistance on his part—and straddled his hips. "Now," she said, giving him a meaningful stare.

"I love a woman who knows her own mind."

Her heart sort of lurched at his statement, but it wasn't a declaration of devotion. Besides, she knew words spoken in passion were not to be taken seriously.

For a second, that fact almost hurt, but it didn't matter, she sternly told the inner longing, she wouldn't *let* it matter, not at this moment.

"I want the magic," she whispered, placing a thousand kisses on his face and neck and chest. "Like before. I want the intensity and…and everything."

"We'll have it," he promised. He fisted his hands in her hair and gently pulled her face to his. "All of it."

And they did—the sweeping passion, the powerful climax, the blissful afterglow. It was everything they'd shared before and more. More, she thought as she drifted into sleep, because there was more….

Chapter Twelve

"Are you awake?"

Zia uncurled herself from Jeremy's arms. It was morning and the rain still came down outside. She didn't want to get out of bed. Bunching a pillow against the headboard, she gave him a dazzling smile, which seemed to take him aback.

"Yes."

He stroked his fingers through her hair. "I'm not sure I didn't, uh, catch you at a weak moment last night. The storm, the phone calls. Why didn't you tell me about those?"

"There was nothing to tell." She deliberately kept her expression bland as he studied her. "And nothing happened between us that I hadn't been dreaming about for days."

He groaned, then laughed and leaned over to kiss her neck before sitting up. "Stay here. I'll get us some coffee."

In a few minutes he returned with a tray, bringing two steaming cups of fresh-brewed coffee, two English muffins with peanut butter and jelly and two glasses of orange juice.

"Breakfast is served," he intoned, sounding like an English butler with a Western drawl.

She laughed, unable to contain her delight. Whatever her questions about the future, she was content at this moment. The mountain storm had chilled the early-morning air, so they snuggled in bed and ate the meal. Jeremy insisted on feeding her, then kissing a smear of jelly off her lips.

It was the most romantic meal she'd ever had.

By the time they'd finished their coffee, she found they were both ready for more intense activity. When he tossed the covers aside and planted a line of kisses all the way down her body to her toes, the room temperature seemed to go up several degrees and become quite comfortable.

"I love the smell of you," he murmured, inhaling deeply, then nuzzling his face against her abdomen.

When he took the caresses to intimate depths, she couldn't suppress the moans of rising desire as she ran her fingers through his hair. In minutes she was impatient for his complete touch, to have them melded into one sweet whole.

When she writhed against him and tugged, he came to her, a smile sparkling in his eyes. "You have to be quieter. It gets me too excited when you scream and moan."

Cupping her hands around his face, she rubbed noses with him. "Yeah? What happens when you're making all the noise?"

She kissed his mouth, his neck and shoulders, all over his chest and worked her way down to his instep and back up. He groaned when she stopped midbody.

In less than a minute, he enclosed her in a tight embrace, rolled to the top position and reached for the bedside drawer.

She sighed when the protection was secure and they at last were merged into one blissful entity. "You make me feel—"

"What?" he demanded, thrusting slowly, deeply. "What do you feel?"

"Desirable," she whispered. "Wanted. Beautiful."

"You are beautiful," he murmured in a deepened tone and gently bit on her earlobe.

"Inside. You make me feel beautiful inside."

He lifted his head and gazed into her eyes. "You are," he said. "More so than I think you know."

Zia stood at the window of the office trailer Wednesday morning and observed the activity around the construction site. The rain had finally stopped last Sunday. The ground had dried out enough that the heavy equipment was back in operation. People and earthmoving machines scurried about, busy as ants on a new hill.

She'd finished all the work she could find to do and waited for the auditor to appear. He'd been there off and on for a couple of weeks, appearing without warning several mornings. He'd also stopped by one afternoon, according to Jeremy, but had quickly left when he'd discovered no one was there to find records and invoices for him and he had to do the work himself.

Shortly after eleven, Marti dropped by to see if she wanted to go to lunch.

"I suppose," she replied. "The auditor hasn't shown up, so I assume he's not coming today."

Sadie waved to them as they headed for the mess tent, then joined them after the dump truck was loaded and on its way.

"It's nice working after the rain," she said, placing her tray on the table next to Zia's. "No dust."

"Give it another three days," Marti said with wry good humor, "and it'll be the same as usual. With fall coming, we'll get more rain, but it'll also be cooler during the working hours. That's always a blessing."

Sadie looked glum.

"What?" Marti asked.

A blush spread over the eighteen-year-old's smooth cheeks. "I have a question," she said in a very low voice after a glance around to make sure no one was close enough to overhear. "How do you know when a person is in love?"

She looked so young and uncertain and appealing that Zia's heart went out to her.

"Well," Marti said on a practical note, "there's all the breathless, shaky, pulse-pounding symptoms."

"That's sex." Sadie wrinkled her nose as if to say the

physical reactions didn't count. "How do you know it's really love, like, deep down in the heart true love?"

Zia found herself waiting anxiously for Marti's answer.

"Only your own heart can tell you for sure," the older woman said, sounding very serious. "It's a question I've been asking myself lately."

Zia's surprise was mirrored in Sadie's face.

Marti laughed softly. "You got any ideas?" she asked Zia.

When both women looked at her, Zia shook her head, then reconsidered. "Maybe…maybe when the need to be with that one person overrides everything else— doubts and qualms and all that."

"Yeah," Sadie murmured as if she knew exactly what Zia was talking about. Her eyes followed the three men who entered the tent at that moment. "What if the other person thinks you're too young to know what love is?"

Gordan, Jeremy and Steve, the engineer who reported to Jeremy and was in charge of the engineering duties of the site on a daily basis, formed a handsome group of masculine camaraderie. For a second, Zia wondered which man the other woman thought she might be in love with.

"Steve?" Marti inquired.

Sadie's blush deepened as she ducked her head and lowered her gaze to her food. "I'll only be here until the end of the month, then I go to the university in Salt Lake."

She sounded as if heading off to college was the same as being banished to Siberia. Just the way Zia had felt when she'd left Idaho to go to college and work for her father in Oregon.

"That's tough," Marti said softly. She thought it over for a few minutes, then said, "Steve's very intelligent. He'll want a wife who's smart and educated. Why not ask if he'd like to write, no, e-mail—that keeps it simple—while you're away? See how it goes from there. You could invite him up for the big homecoming weekend during football season or something like that. If he accepts, then maybe you two have something going that will last while you get your schooling in. Only time will tell."

That sounded so wise. Zia wondered how she could apply the same reasoning to herself.

"What about you and Gordan?" Sadie demanded, recovering her sassy spirit that somehow wasn't obnoxious.

"Ah, that would be telling," Marti quipped. "Actually, I think we're both sort of testing the water. He's been divorced, so he's wary of marriage. I have two kids to consider, so that's another complication. I'm content to take things slow and easy for the present."

"That's a good idea," Zia said. "People tend to rush into relationships. Maybe love, like fine wine, needs time to develop its full potential."

When Marti and Sadie studied her in an interested fashion, as if waiting to hear more, Zia managed a smile and a shrug.

"But don't ask me. I'm no expert," she concluded.

She was very glad when the three men joined them and the conversation changed to road construction.

* * *

On Thursday, Zia arrived at the office at eight as usual. Jeremy was in town for meetings that morning. The site workers had been on the job since seven and would work until dark. The extra overtime had been approved by the DOT earlier that month.

She waved to Marti, who operated a crane and guided heavy lengths of rebar into place where the concrete base would be poured, and to Sadie, who directed traffic with the confidence born from nearly three months of experience.

Zia released a long, contented sigh. Things were going well on all fronts. Remembering the previous weekend, she amended that thought. Things were heavenly.

Last Saturday, after they finally got out of bed, Jeremy had built a fire to ward off the chill of the mountain storm and they had basked in its warmth all weekend. The hours had been spent reading and making love, watching TV and making love, cooking, eating…making love….

She'd never felt so sated and happy and at peace inside.

It won't last, a part of her warned.

Well, yes, she knew that. Nothing, good or bad, lasted forever. She knew not to expect too much, not to dream too big. Slow and easy, as Marti had said. That was her philosophy.

Careerwise, things were moving along. The head of the school board had informed her the state was coming through with the promised funds, although it would be January before the money arrived. She would have a full-time position in the new year.

Tina had indicated her mom would tend to the baby and she could return to work part-time at the construction office when Zia left.

So all was well. Smiling, she went inside and hurried to the desk when the phone rang.

"Hey," a deep raspy voice said.

Every nerve in her body tensed. The irritating calls had stopped at the cottage since Jeremy had put a counterblock on those whose phone numbers weren't available. Had the caller now discovered where she worked?

She started to hang up without speaking, then reconsidered. This was the office, and the call was likely about business. "Who is this?" she asked coldly.

"Smitty. How ya doing?"

"Fine," she snapped, none too friendly.

"Jeremy asked me to check on some calls you've been getting. I wanted to let you know we've got the guy. Some sheriff's deputies are on their way to arrest him as we speak."

"Really?" she said in surprise.

"Yep. After I put out an alert, we learned he'd been pestering several women in the area. We put tracers on two phones and ran him down."

"That's great," she said with a lot more warmth.

"Uh, listen. I'm sorry about coming on to you that night at Jeremy's. I was just, well, sort of bowled over at finding a movie star in his kitchen and I acted on impulse. A *stupid* impulse."

She laughed. "Movie star? Hardly."

"Actually, I thought I'd stumbled onto an angel. I

wanted to grab you before one of the other guys did and take you home with me. Not a good idea, huh?"

"I don't usually go home with guys at the first meeting," she told him in a wry tone.

"I'm surprised ol' Jere didn't deck me."

"Nah, he assured me you were harmless." She paused. "Just now, when I answered the phone, I thought you might be the caller. You have a deep voice, the same as he does."

"Damn, Zia, I'm sorry about that."

He sounded so sincerely concerned that she instantly forgave him for the kitchen incident. "I'm glad you found out who the man was. He kept asking if I was alone, like he might show up if I answered in the affirmative. It was creepy. I always hung up without speaking."

"You did right not to answer him. No response usually gets rid of scum like that. They get their kicks by scaring people."

After they rang off, she sat down at the desk and began sorting through the reports Jeremy had previously dropped off. The repair at the double-S curve would take a month, she saw. That meant he would have to shift equipment away from this job for that length of time.

She wondered if that would disrupt the newly planned schedule for the bridge construction. At least in her job she didn't have to contend with weather as well as the vagaries of school boards and state governments.

"Ready for lunch?" Marti asked an hour later, sticking her head in the trailer door.

Zia rose and stretched her back. "I'm ready."

At the mess tent, the two women sat with Sadie. Gordan joined them. Ten minutes later, Jeremy came in. Zia couldn't stop the fevered pounding of her heart as he filled a tray and came over.

Recalling that Sadie had dismissed the reaction as merely physical, she forced a calm she was far from feeling at his unexpected appearance.

Since she sat at the end of the table with Marti to her left, he sat across the table from her, next to Sadie. His foot nudged hers in a playful private greeting. He grinned when she gave him a startled glance.

Gordan waggled his eyebrows at Marti. "Jeremy and I have decided to splurge and take you gals out for dinner and dancing tomorrow night. Sadie, you got a date?"

"I can get one," she assured him. "Since Jeremy isn't available." She cut her gaze from him to Zia, then grinned.

Zia felt the heat flow up her neck and hoped she wasn't bright red. She gave the younger woman a nonchalant smile.

Jeremy gave a little yank on Sadie's ponytail. "I stay away from you femme fatales."

Zia laughed when the others did, but the sound echoed through the chambers of her heart. The yearning, which had seemed far away all week, suddenly returned. Her heart pounded even harder, as if it wanted to tell her something.

"That's it," Mr. Ling told her on Friday shortly before noon.

The auditor had been in twice that week, each time

arriving unannounced. Zia fetched records and reports as directed while he compared them to information in his laptop computer.

"Are we finished?" she asked.

"We are."

His sudden smile, the first she'd gotten from him, caused her to blink in surprise. She smiled, too, and wanted to ask if they had passed the audit, but she stifled her curiosity. Sooner or later, a long report would be generated and sent out, informing Jeremy of the office bookkeeping skills, or lack thereof. As far as she could tell, the accounts were in order.

"Thank you for your help," Mr. Ling said in his formal way.

"No problem," she assured him. "We have to account for every penny in the educational programs, too. Which is good," she added so he wouldn't think she was complaining.

They talked about the new curriculum program—he had two children in high school, he told her—while he stored the computer in his briefcase and checked that he had everything.

After he left, Zia quickly replaced the bills of lading and the records in the files. Even if she skipped lunch, she was going to be late for her afternoon job, but she would stay over to make up the time. She didn't want to leave any loose ends here over the weekend. It was nearly one when she finished the task, grabbed her purse and headed out the door.

The annoying ping of a truck backing up assailed her

ears when she paused on the steps. She smiled as Sadie waved the dump truck driver into position to take on a load of dirt.

Directly beyond the truck, she could see the boom of the biggest on-site crane as it swung a huge steel beam into place to form part of the bridge base. It seemed to Zia that the truck was backing toward the crane and that the two were awfully close to each other.

Her breath caught in her throat. She realized Sadie couldn't see the crane on the other side of the truck and that Marti, concentrating on the beam placement, didn't see the truck coming toward her.

"Stop!" Zia yelled. "Sadie, stop!"

She realized she couldn't be heard over the general noise in the area. Leaping from the top step, she hit the ground running, her arms waving to catch Sadie's attention.

But even if she'd been a track star, she knew she couldn't get to them in time. The truck driver was watching Sadie while he backed up and Sadie was watching the distance close between the truck and the crawler-loader. The crane was in their blind spot.

From the corner of her eye, she caught sight of a vehicle approaching. Jeremy came straight at her, then threw on the brakes when he came close. He stopped beside her in a whirl of dust.

"What is it?" he asked.

"The dump truck. Stop it. The crane—"

He took off, blowing the horn like a madman.

Too late. She saw the boom on the crane bounce, then

swing in a wide arc and disappear. Sadie dropped her flags and ran. The driver cut the truck engine and bounded down just as Zia passed him. Together, they joined the crew rushing to the scene of the accident. Engines shut down and only the whirr of the crane motor disturbed the sudden quiet.

"Marti," Sadie cried. "Help her. Somebody help her."

"Hush," Gordan said harshly, running past them. He joined Jeremy at the edge of the gorge where the crane tipped precariously over the edge, its boom now entangled in a broken steel cable supporting the footbridge. The steel beam swung like a pendulum over the rushing waters of the river.

Two rafts, each holding six people, stopped at the bank several yards beyond the site to see what was happening.

Zia stood beside Sadie and put an arm around her shoulders. The younger woman gasped as the soft earth gave way and the side of the crane leaned over the edge a bit more. A whole section of dirt had given way beneath the machine.

There was no answer when Gordan shouted at Marti. "She must have hit her head," he said. "She's not moving."

"We need a couple of chains with hooks," Jeremy said. "Sadie, get that truck turned around. We'll hook it to the crane and pull it to safety. Cam, get the D-11 over here. We'll need it, too."

Zia knew from the reports she'd read that the D-ll was the largest dozer on-site, a monster with tank tracks instead of tires because of the rough terrain.

"Go," she whispered to Sadie. "Marti needs you. Go."

The truck driver and Sadie, tear tracks on her face, resumed their jobs. When the truck and dozer were in position, Cam and Gordan saw to securing the chains.

"Easy," Jeremy shouted to the drivers when the other men indicated they were ready. "Sadie, back 'em up."

Pointing a flag at each driver, Sadie directed them to start moving slowly and in unison as Jeremy called out directions. Zia was proud of the girl's composure.

The crane began to move, then stopped as the boom jerked and bounced up and down.

"The footbridge cables are in the way," Cam told Jeremy. "We need to ease out the line holding the beam as the crane moves back, or else we'll have to use enough force to break the rest of the cables."

Zia heard Jeremy mutter a curse. He, Cam and Gordan walked to the footbridge and studied the situation. "I think you're right," Jeremy said after a brief discussion. He directed Cam to take over and strode toward the precariously leaning crane.

When Zia realized he was going to climb on the piece of heavy equipment, her heart leaped to her throat, stopping the cry of protest as he swung up on the machine and made his way to the cab.

Marti slumped into his arms when he opened the door.

Zia saw Gordan glance once at them, then check the tension on the thick chains holding the crane in place and nod to Cam that he was ready. Jeremy reached across Marti and shifted a lever, easing the tension off the cable holding the steel beam.

At Cam's command, Sadie again pointed at each

driver, then directed them to move away from the gorge. The dozer driver's job was to maintain an even tension on the chain while the truck pulled the crane back from the chasm. Now, as movement began again, Jeremy let the line out at an even rate to stop the footbridge from moving, too.

Although it seemed an eternity, only five minutes crawled by as the crane was eased back from the brink of disaster.

Then it was over.

Shouts broke out as several men rushed forward, but it was Gordan who was there first to put his arms around Marti when Jeremy helped her from the cab. Blood ran down the side of her face where she'd hit her head.

"I'm okay," she said, dazed but able to stand.

"We'll let the doctor make that decision," Gordan told her, leading the way to his pickup.

When Jeremy jumped to the ground, his eyes met Zia's. She gave him a furious glare and turned away. Heading for her car, she noticed Sadie was in Cam's arms, sobbing her heart out after the tense moments. Zia knew how she felt.

Jeremy hadn't sent one of the other heavy equipment drivers into the crane while it was tilted over the edge of the gorge. Although the danger at that point, with the truck and crawler-loader holding the crane, was minimized, it was still a frightening situation. Jeremy wouldn't ask more of another person than he was willing to do.

While he gave orders to the crew and they resumed

work, Zia hurried to her car. Her hands shook so badly she could hardly fit the key into the ignition and drive the winding road into town for her afternoon job. She couldn't get the tense moments out of her mind.

The dangerous incident had ended safely for everyone but her.

Seeing Jeremy in the perilous situation had forced her to see the truth, which her heart had known for ages—she had let herself come to depend on him...for happiness, for the contentment of sharing their lives, for all the needs of her heart....

Chapter Thirteen

Jeremy reported the accident by phone to his boss at the main DOT office. Since no one was injured and no equipment repair was needed, there was no reason to write up an accident report.

He smiled grimly. The boss had cut him and the crew some slack there. Man, if Marti had been seriously hurt, the paperwork would have been never-ending. The big crane had a newly rebuilt engine and was worth over half a million smackaroos. If they'd lost that over the gorge, he would have been digging ditches at the bottom of the Grand Canyon for the rest of his career.

One good thing—the head honchos now understood the problem with the unstable earth at the site had not been exaggerated. They were going to have to reinforce the support piers with more concrete and rebar.

He left the office and drove home at a reasonable speed, reasonable because he wanted to floor the pedal and get to Zia as fast as the SUV would go, but he stayed within the speed limit, or thereabouts.

An image of her face when she'd left the bridge site appeared in his inner vision. Ashen skin. Eyes like bruised petals.

Naturally she'd been frightened for Marti, and maybe a little for him, although there hadn't been any danger of toppling over the edge at that point. At any rate, he wanted to assure her that all was well.

The sight of the cottage caused his heart to jolt as if it had gone over a speed bump. Actually, the occupant was what caused his insides to go off balance. He grinned. Zia had a way of doing that to him.

And to other men, like Smitty, who'd been captured by her beauty from the first moment, then by her charm and gratitude after the cops had nabbed the frightening caller.

Inside, he found her sitting in the sunroom, a sandwich and a glass of tea on the table beside her.

"Hey, we're supposed to go out to dinner tonight," he reminded her, bending down for the kiss he'd come to expect.

She turned her head slightly so the kiss landed at the corner of her mouth. "Marti called. She has a slight concussion, so she and Gordan won't be going out tonight."

"We could still go. A lot of the crew will be there."

"I'd rather not. I have a headache."

He dropped to his haunches and propped his elbow on the arm of her chair. "Is the accident still bothering you? Everything's fine, nobody hurt, no equipment lost."

"Yes, I know. You and Gordan and Cam did a magnificent job of getting things under control. Will anything happen to Sadie?"

He gave her a puzzled glance. "It wasn't Sadie's fault."

Now it was Zia's turn to look confused. "Didn't she cause the truck to back into the crane? I saw the boom swing out over the gorge and I thought—"

"No, no," he interrupted. "The earth suddenly slumped. You recall we were having problems with soft pockets?" At her nod, he continued, "Marti hit her head and jerked the control stick, which in turn caused the beam to swing out and hit the footbridge, becoming entangled in its cables and snapping one of them. It was just one of those unpredictable things that happen."

A relieved smile appeared on her beautiful face. "I was so worried about Sadie."

That odd tenderness filled his chest. "Did you think we would boil her in oil or something?"

"No, just throw her in a dungeon for a hundred years."

They laughed together.

"I'm still on for dinner and dancing. I feel like holding a lovely woman in my arms while the rest of the guys drool in their beer."

She hesitated, then nodded.

"Let's get ready then. I'm starved. I need to take a quick shower."

A few minutes later, with the warm water flowing

over his body, he reflected on the tension he sensed in Zia. Maybe she was strung up because of the bozo who'd frightened her with the calls, then the auditor had been in and out all week; add to that the drama with Marti, who had become a close friend. Maybe that had been the final straw for Zia. Maybe the evening out would be good for her—

At that moment, the shower door opened.

"May I?" Zia asked politely, a smile tugging at the corners of her lips. She was totally, beautifully nude.

His mouth went dry, his brain went soft and all the blood in his body went south. "You may," he murmured, reaching for her.

The dancing had started by the time they joined their friends at the tavern.

On Sunday, Zia took the classified section of the paper, her cell phone and a fresh cup of coffee to the sunroom right after breakfast. Her usual Sunday routine.

She sighed as she flipped open the pages. There were few listings, and it didn't take her fifteen minutes to skim through all the houses for sale or rent, and the apartments.

The apartment at the widow's home that had sounded promising last month was listed again. She had the same problem with it—her furniture would have to stay at Jeremy's place or in storage.

So what was so bad about that?

With things working out with the job, she could afford the storage fees while she shopped for a more permanent home.

Her heart clenched so hard she thought she just might be having a heart attack…well, she was, but not a physical one.

Glancing toward the perimeter of the yard, she watched as Jeremy worked on the underbrush along the edge of the woods.

She had to leave his cottage, this haven where she'd found the greatest peace she'd ever known. She'd realized that Friday when she'd thought he was in danger.

It was the idea that he could have been hurt that drove her to despair. That, and the realization that she loved him with all her being.

How had that happened?

It had sneaked up on her so quietly, so gently, she hadn't realized it was coming. She'd thought she could seize the moment, so to speak, and that she'd known what she was doing.

Picking up her cell phone, she called the widow's number. "Mrs. Whitcomb? This is Zia Peters. I stopped by and looked at the apartment at your place last month. Is it still available?"

It was, so Zia asked if it was okay to come by after lunch and look at it again. She explained the problem of her furniture and that she would eventually need a larger place.

The widow assured her that the rental was monthly, rather than on a lease basis, and that she could leave with thirty days notice.

"I'll see you later then."

Satisfied that this was the right thing to do, Zia manicured her nails and painted both her toenails and fingernails a bright pink, then put on pink linen slacks with a lacy white top.

When Jeremy came in shortly before noon, he stopped in his tracks. "Wow, you look like a luscious strawberry," he told her, his smile brighter than sunshine to her. "I may have to take a bite or two."

"If you want lunch, you'd better wash up." She grinned as she squeezed a few drops of mustard over corned beef and cabbage in a random pattern, then took the plates to the table.

He washed up and quickly returned, holding a chair for her, then stealing a kiss on the back of her neck before taking his seat. "Now this is a meal after a man's heart," he declared, helping himself to hot corn bread squares.

The restless sadness—the same as she'd felt after going home for the wedding—attached itself to her spirit, sucking out the contentment she'd found here like a leech bent on destroying her soul.

"I was thinking of a hike up the ridge this afternoon," he said, "but you're dressed pretty fancy. Would you like to go to a movie instead?"

She shook her head. "I, uh, have an appointment." She cleared her throat. "I'm going to look at an apartment in town. Mrs. Whitcomb is a widow who rents out two rooms in her house. The apartment has its own bath and a private entrance."

When she glanced at Jeremy, the smile was gone and

his face was utterly still. It could have been a painting for all the life in his expression.

"Isn't that one of the places you mentioned a few weeks ago?" he asked in an oddly soft tone that sent a chill along her spine. "The one that was furnished?"

"Yes. Now that my job is on again, I can afford to keep everything in storage until I find a house or larger place." She spoke in a cheerful fashion, as if everything was working out just the way she wanted.

Yeah, just peachy.

Tears burned her eyes and she felt precariously on edge as he studied her for a moment. "I see," he said.

They finished the meal in silence. He looked thoughtful and introspective while she tried to appear casual and composed.

"The woods look nice where you've cleared the brush away. I'm glad that big patch of poison oak is gone. It has such blazing color in the fall I would have probably brought some inside and put it in a vase without realizing what it was." Her laughter sounded hollow.

"Yeah, it is pretty."

His gaze lingered on her for a moment, then returned to his plate. When they finished, she asked if he'd like a dish of ice cream for dessert.

"No, thanks."

He took his dishes to the dishwasher, then stood by the counter while she stored the leftovers in the fridge.

"Well," she said, glancing at the clock, "I had better get on the road. Is there anything you need in town while I'm there?"

"Not that I can think of."

"Well," she said again, not sure what to do as he continued standing in the way so she would have had to squeeze by him to leave.

"Zia—"

She looked at him with a question in her eyes.

"Uh, nothing."

He stepped aside and she quickly got her purse from the credenza. With the car keys in her hand, she headed for the carport. When she started to push the screened door open, his voice, low and husky, made her pause.

"You don't have to leave."

She faced him, her heartbeat a muted *whack* that nearly rocked her body with each thud. "I think I have to." Her throat closed up and she had to swallow. "It would be too easy to…to get into a rut and miss an opportunity to find the perfect place."

"Yeah," he said. "That would be too bad."

"Yes." She stood there like a statue, but unlike cold stone, she ached inside. The stupid tears pushed against her control. She had to get out of there…had to…

"Zia?" In two strides, he stood in front of her, a concerned frown on his face. "What is it?"

"Nothing," she managed to choke out.

He leaned closer and stared into her face. "Are you crying?"

"No, of course not." But as she shook her head in adamant denial, two fat tears broke free and rolled down her face.

No, no, no, she ordered the wayward tears, but it was

no use. She covered her face, the car keys pressing into her cheek, and shook her head again.

"Zia," he murmured, then he wrapped his arms around her and pulled her close, surrounding her with his warmth and strength and caring nature.

"Oh, don't," she cried. "I can't stand it."

He dropped his arms as if burned. "You can't stand my touch?" he said in shocked tones.

"No, I can't stand to go." She was horrified as the truth poured out. "I can't stand to stay, either."

"This isn't making a lot of sense to me. Could you be a little plainer?"

Blinking away the ridiculous tears that kept seeping out against her will, she stared into his dark eyes with their intriguing green flecks. "Things are getting too complicated. Between us. It's so wonderful here. And that's why I have to leave." She gave a helpless moan. "Oh, God, that makes no sense at all."

He reached out and caressed the tears off her cheek. "Maybe it does. Maybe this is the first time anything has made sense between us." He cupped her face and stepped closer. "Let's tell the truth before we make a mistake that will forever change our lives."

"What mistake?"

"Giving each other up because we think we have to."

"We do—"

"No," he contradicted. "We don't. We can have everything we've had the past few weeks and more."

Her heart stopped, just stopped. "More what?"

He gave her the tiniest brush of a kiss. "That. All the

things we've shared lately. Working together. Eating. Dancing." His voice dropped to almost inaudible levels. "Making love."

She couldn't speak, could only stare at him, this man that she loved more than any other.

"Making love," he repeated as if he found the idea filled with wonder. "It is love, isn't it?" He nodded before she could agree. "That's what I feel. That's why I was so anxious to get home every night, knowing you were here and would soon be in my arms. Love, Zia. For you."

"Jeremy," she whispered as shock and delight filled her to the bursting point. "Oh, Jeremy."

Somehow they became all entwined, his thigh pressing between hers, their arms holding each other as tightly as possible, their lips...their hearts....

They shared the sweetest kisses, until both were breathless, until she felt as if she would melt at his feet. "My knees are weak," she said when he kissed her neck.

He swept her into his arms. In fifteen seconds, they were on the sofa, stretched out with not a smidgen of air between them. It was a long, long time before they could pick up the discussion again.

"I love you," he said. "I think I have for aeons without knowing it."

The words trembled on her tongue, so hard to say, yet impossible to hold in. "I love you, too." She pressed her face into his neck. "It scares me."

Jeremy heard the barely whispered words and a whole armada of invisible darts hit his heart. He knew how difficult it had been for her to say it. Her trust had been shaken years ago, when her father left, he thought, then again when her former steady had betrayed her trust.

"I would never hurt you," he assured her.

She lifted her head. Her eyes were damp, but shining, reminding him of flowers after a summer rain.

"I know that," she told him, her hands roaming over his chest in a manner that turned him on. "I thought I had to leave because I was beginning to depend on you. I thought I shouldn't because whatever we had was temporary."

He brought her hand to his lips and kissed the palm. "Not on your life. We're forever, you and I."

Zia heard his soft laughter, saw the happiness in his eyes, felt his love in every touch. She laughed, too, as joy filled her heart and her soul basked in the warmth.

They kissed and murmured things to each other, each wanting to know what the other had felt and when.

"Krista's wedding," she confessed. "It confused me. And when we danced, I felt odd, disoriented. Frightened."

"The wedding," he murmured. "That was the turning point." He gazed deeply into her eyes. "When are we going to have ours? We've wasted enough time. I want it to be soon."

She nodded. "We'll have to call the folks—"

He grinned at her sudden stop. "You think they suspected this might happen when we both moved here?"

"I think my mom might have wished it," she said, snuggling in his arms as contentment flooded through her.

Her statement was proved true when they called Jeff and Caileen later that afternoon—long after Zia had canceled her appointment with the widow.

"Jeremy," her mom said in great delight, "was exactly the person I would have chosen for you."

After discussing possible wedding dates, Zia replaced the phone. Jeremy gave her a troubled glance.

"What?" she asked.

"I hope your mom's approval doesn't make you have second thoughts about us."

Laughing, she dived into his arms and buried herself right up to her heart in his sweet love.

"I used to be a defiant teenager," she admitted. "But now I'm much wiser."

"Yeah?"

"Yeah. I fell for you, didn't I?"

His lips hovered over hers. "We were both wise," he whispered. "I opened my home to you. You opened your heart to me. I got a bargain out of the deal."

"Home," she repeated. "It takes two hearts to make it real."

"You got it," he murmured.

Discussion over.

* * * * *

Happily ever after is just the beginning...

Turn the page for a sneak preview of
DANCING ON SUNDAY AFTERNOONS
by
Linda Cardillo

Harlequin Everlasting—Every great love
has a story to tell. ™
A brand-new line from Harlequin Books
launching this February!

Prologue

Giulia D'Orazio
1983

I had two husbands—Paolo and Salvatore.

Salvatore and I were married for thirty-two years. I still live in the house he bought for us; I still sleep in our bed. All around me are the signs of our life together. My bedroom window looks out over the garden he planted. In the middle of the city, he coaxed tomatoes, peppers, zucchini—even grapes for his wine—out of the ground. On weekends, he used to drive up to his cousin's farm in Waterbury and bring back manure. In the winter, he wrapped the peach tree and the fig tree with rags and black rubber hoses against the cold, his massive, coarse hands gentling those trees as if they were his fragile-skinned babies. My neighbor, Dominic Grazza, does that for me now. My boys have no time for the garden.

In the front of the house, Salvatore planted roses. The roses I take care of myself. They are giant, cream-colored, fragrant. In the afternoons, I like to sit out on the porch with my coffee, protected from the eyes of the neighborhood by that curtain of flowers.

Salvatore died in this house thirty-five years ago. In the last months, he lay on the sofa in the parlor so he could be in the middle of everything. Except for the two oldest boys, all the children were still at home and we ate together every evening. Salvatore could see the dining room table from the sofa, and he could hear everything that was said. "I'm not dead, yet," he told me. "I want to know what's going on."

When my first grandchild, Cara, was born, we brought her to him, and he held her on his chest, stroking her tiny head. Sometimes they fell asleep together.

Over on the radiator cover in the corner of the parlor is the portrait Salvatore and I had taken on our twenty-fifth anniversary. This brooch I'm wearing today, with the diamonds—I'm wearing it in the photograph also— Salvatore gave it to me that day. Upstairs on my dresser is a jewelry box filled with necklaces and bracelets and earrings. All from Salvatore.

I am surrounded by the things Salvatore gave me, or

did for me. But, God forgive me, as I lie alone now in my bed, it is Paolo I remember.

Paolo left me nothing. Nothing, that is, that my family, especially my sisters, thought had any value. No house. No diamonds. Not even a photograph.

But after he was gone, and I could catch my breath from the pain, I knew that I still had something. In the middle of the night, I sat alone and held them in my hands, reading the words over and over until I heard his voice in my head. I had Paolo's letters.

* * * * *

Be sure to look for
DANCING ON SUNDAY AFTERNOONS
available January 30, 2007.
And look, too, for our other
Everlasting title available,
FALL FROM GRACE by Kristi Gold.

FALL FROM GRACE is a deeply emotional story
of what a long-term love really means.
As Jack and Anne Morgan discover, marriage vows
can be broken—but they can be mended, too.
And the memories of their marriage have an
unexpected power to bring back a love
that never really left....

HARLEQUIN® *Romance*®

What a month!

In February watch for

Rancher and Protector
Part of the Western Weddings miniseries
BY JUDY CHRISTENBERRY

The Boss's Pregnancy Proposal
BY RAYE MORGAN

Also in February, expect
MORE of what you love
as the Harlequin Romance line
increases to six titles per month.

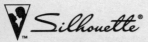

HARLEQUIN®
Super Romance®

Is it really possible to find true love
when you're single…with kids?

Introducing an exciting new five-book miniseries,

SINGLES…WITH KIDS

When Margo almost loses her bistro…and custody of
her children…she realizes a real family is about more
than owning a pretty house and being a perfect mother.
And then there's the new man in her life, Robert…
Like the other single parents in her support group, she
has to make sure he wants the whole package.

Starting in February 2007 with

LOVE AND THE SINGLE MOM
by C.J. Carmichael
(Harlequin Superromance #1398)

ALSO WATCH FOR:

THE SISTER SWITCH Pamela Ford (#1404, on sale March 2007)
ALL-AMERICAN FATHER Anna DeStefano (#1410, on sale April 2007)
THE BEST-KEPT SECRET Melinda Curtis (#1416, on sale May 2007)
BLAME IT ON THE DOG Amy Frazier (#1422, on sale June 2007)

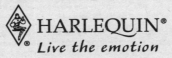

HARLEQUIN®
Live the emotion

REQUEST YOUR FREE BOOKS!
2 FREE NOVELS PLUS 2 FREE GIFTS!

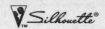

SPECIAL EDITION®
Life, Love and Family!

YES! Please send me 2 FREE Silhouette Special Edition® novels and my 2 FREE gifts. After receiving them, if I don't wish to receive any more books, I can return the shipping statement marked "cancel." If I don't cancel, I will receive 6 brand-new novels every month and be billed just $4.24 per book in the U.S., or $4.99 per book in Canada, plus 25¢ shipping and handling per book and applicable taxes, if any*. That's a savings of at least 15% off the cover price! I understand that accepting the 2 free books and gifts places me under no obligation to buy anything. I can always return a shipment and cancel at any time. Even if I never buy another book from Silhouette, the two free books and gifts are mine to keep forever. 235 SDN EEYU 335 SDN EEY6

Name	(PLEASE PRINT)	
Address		Apt.
City	State/Prov.	Zip/Postal Code

Signature (if under 18, a parent or guardian must sign)

Mail to the Silhouette Reader Service™:
IN U.S.A.: P.O. Box 1867, Buffalo, NY 14240-1867
IN CANADA: P.O. Box 609, Fort Erie, Ontario L2A 5X3

Not valid to current Silhouette Special Edition subscribers.

Want to try two free books from another line?
Call 1-800-873-8635 or visit www.morefreebooks.com.

* Terms and prices subject to change without notice. NY residents add applicable sales tax. Canadian residents will be charged applicable provincial taxes and GST. This offer is limited to one order per household. All orders subject to approval. Credit or debit balances in a customer's account(s) may be offset by any other outstanding balance owed by or to the customer. Please allow 4 to 6 weeks for delivery.

Your Privacy: Silhouette is committed to protecting your privacy. Our Privacy Policy is available online at www.eHarlequin.com or upon request from the Reader Service. From time to time we make our lists of customers available to reputable firms who may have a product or service of interest to you. If you would prefer we not share your name and address, please check here. ☐

SSE07

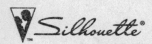
Silhouette®

COMING NEXT MONTH

#1807 FALLING FOR THE TEXAS TYCOON—
Karen Rose Smith
Logan's Legacy Revisited
Skilled at guarding her boss's schedule, twenty-one-year-old office manager Lisa Sanders also had to guard her own heart when Texas real estate mogul Alan Barrett showed up one day without an appointment. But would the secrets of Lisa's wild teenage years derail a runaway romance with this self-assured older man?

#1808 THE PRODIGAL VALENTINE—Karen Templeton
Babies, Inc.
When Ben Vargas returned to Albuquerque to help out with his father's construction business, he was confused as ever about his place in the family and the community. One thing was certain—reuniting with his former flame, sassy shop owner Mercedes Zamora, was a top priority. But would Mercy still want to be his valentine after all these years?

#1809 THE BRIDESMAID'S GIFTS—Gina Wilkins
Businessman Ethan Brannon was in Cabot, Arkansas, to act as best man in his brother's wedding—not to listen to the psychic mumbo jumbo of bridesmaid Aislinn Flaherty. But when Aislinn offered him new hope about an old family tragedy, Ethan had a vision of his own about this compassionate woman and her very special gifts.

#1810 JUST FRIENDS?—Allison Leigh
When producer Leandra Clay enlisted her old friend, veterinarian Evan Taggart, to be on her reality TV series, it was a good match— they were both known to throw themselves into their work. But soon they were throwing themselves into each other's arms...until the show aired, and they suddenly found themselves fending off Evan's female fans!

#1811 THE MARRIAGE SOLUTION—Brenda Harlen
Career woman Tess Lucas knew the night of passion with her best friend, pharmaceutical exec Craig Richmond, was a mistake. Now she had proof—she was pregnant. Yet Tess declined Craig's marriage offer, reasoning their friendship wouldn't survive a thing like *marriage*. Then Craig refused her refusal, and the battle was on....

#1812 FINDING HIS WAY HOME—Barbara Gale
Years ago, heiress Valetta Faraday had fled the family drama of her privileged California upbringing and forged a new path as a reporter in upstate New York. But now Lincoln Cameron was on a mission to bring her back. Would the pretty widow turn the tables and persuade the L.A. playboy to share her small-town life instead?

SSECNM0107